3 1969 02383 3790

Diversion Books
A Division of Diversion Publishing Corp.
443 Park Avenue South, Suite 1008
New York, New York 10016
www.DiversionBooks.com

For more information, email info@diversionbooks.com

First Diversion Books edition July 2015.
Print ISBN: 978-1-62681-551-3
eBook ISBN: 978-1-62681-550-6

SIGHT

THE DELTA GIRLS: BOOK ONE

JULIET MADISON

DIVERSIONBOOKS

To my sisters-in-writing,
Alli Sinclair and Diane Curran.

CHAPTER 1

I always thought I'd spend my sixteenth birthday at home with my four sisters and closest friends having the sleepover of all sleepovers with streamers and balloons overtaking the living room, a bottomless bowl of salt and vinegar potato chips, and enough chocolate to feed a small country. We'd watch movies, pausing occasionally to drool over hot actors, before turning up the music and dancing around like lunatics. My eldest sister, Talia, and her twin, Tamara, would probably bring out their Ouija board and freak the crap out of all of us. With our nervous systems on high alert for an impending ghost visitation, it'd be more like a *no sleepover*. Add the fuel of excess sugar and hormones to the fire of fear, and we'd be up all night for sure.

Instead, I spent my birthday fast asleep. In a coma, to be exact. Not exactly the picture I had in mind, and I doubt the picture my sisters had in mind either. As the youngest child in the family, everyone always treated me as though I was made of fragile glass; and as one of triplets, my birthday parties were always shared with Serena and Sasha. But, for the momentous occasion of my sweet sixteenth, we were separated by my inconvenient lack of consciousness. Not so sweet after all.

I wasn't aware of my birthday taking place, or aware of anything for that matter. I only remembered the heavy, drowsy sensation after the anesthesiologist put the mask on my face, and then everything around me faded to black. It was a risky operation, no doubt about that. I'd been given the choice of living my life with the ticking time bomb of a brain aneurysm, or having surgery to hopefully repair the damn thing, giving me the possibility of a so-called *normal* life. As any teenager would have done, I reached for the hope of a normal life—that Holy Grail of adolescence and the need to fit in, to be accepted, and to figure out who the heck I was. The idea of walking around with a head that could explode at any minute was about as appealing as wearing the pink sweater with a trail of fluffy pom-poms down each sleeve that Grandma knitted me two Christmas's earlier.

I was told to expect a shocking headache on waking after the operation, but what I didn't expect was not waking up at all. There was no headache, no lights, and no doctors and nurses hovering around me—okay, there could have been, but I wasn't aware of them. I was trapped in a prison of darkness with no way out.

That was until the fourteenth of April, two months after being wheeled into the operating room, when a strange jolt coursed through my body. Warmth flushed my skin, and a kind of *bubbly* sensation tickled me from the inside; and for the first time in a long while, I saw something. The image was as clear as day; I knew it was real.

And then I opened my eyes.

• • •

"Did you feel that?"

"I thought I heard…"

The sound of my sisters' voices became apparent as light soaked into my aching eyes, drowning in a thick blur of white.

"Oh my God. Savannah!"

"Quick, someone get Mom!"

I wanted so much to sit up and hug them, feel that I was indeed alive, but my muscles were deaf to my brain's commands. At least my ears weren't. The mismatched symphony of sounds gnawed at my eardrums, but I didn't care. I was alive. My family was with me. The familiar click-clack of my mother's shoes grew near, followed by her soft breath and cold palm on my face before it was quickly replaced by a sharp light protruding into my eyes.

"Savannah, can you hear me?" an unfamiliar male voice asked. "Blink twice if you can hear me."

I blinked. Twice.

"She really is awake! Honey, it's Mom. Everything's going to be all right."

"I…know." It was as though I was speaking for the first time. The words sounded like strangers hijacking my throat as it scratched and strained in effort. It felt weird, but at the same time, it felt pretty awesome.

• • •

THREE MONTHS LATER

I'd forgotten how delicious ice cream was. Since my operation, eating ice cream had always been rewarded with a sharp, cold headache, but not today. Today I was rewarded with the bliss of boysenberry ripple cooling my tongue and delivering a burst of sweetness to my eager taste buds. I wiped at globs of ice cream as they dripped down my chin and giggled. Serena, my older sister by two and a half minutes, eyed me strangely.

"What?" I asked.

"Huh? Oh, nothing." She flicked her slender hand. "It's just good to hear you laugh again, that's all."

Smiling, I stepped onto the beach, reveling in the luscious, warm sand oozing between my toes. People laughed and chatted around us, children squealed and giggled, and seagulls squawked overhead; all relishing the freedom of the summer holidays. Flags marking the safe section of beach in which to swim flapped in the breeze as lifeguards watched over the crowd. The five of us dawdled along, licking our ice creams and inhaling the salty ocean air that tickled our skin as it swept around us.

Talia stopped and glanced at her feet, her wavy locks tumbling over her shoulders.

"What is it?" we asked in unison.

Bewilderment creasing her face, Talia raised her head. "I don't know. But being here…it reminds me of something." As though giving up trying to figure out what that *something* was, she shrugged, causing a spaghetti strap from her maxi dress to fall off one of her tanned shoulders. She returned it to its rightful position and we continued walking.

A dull thud knocked my head sideways a tad. "Hey!" My gaze darted to the beach volleyballers nearby who were now missing a ball. I tucked the tip of my foot under the offending item, sharply flicked it up, and caught it in one hand. Good to know my soccer skills hadn't died along with the aneurysm. "I'd say that shot was out," I called across to the group of golden-skinned teenagers.

"Ya think?" a boy about my age, maybe older, replied. His hand shaded his face, but when he removed it to reveal beautifully proportioned perfection, I almost dropped the ball. And the ice cream.

Gulp. Maybe moving here away from my friends wasn't so bad after all.

"So, are you gonna give it back or what?" He frowned. "Or can't you throw that far?"

I'd spoken too soon. *What an ass.*

"Here, hold this." I thrust my half-eaten ice cream cone into Talia's unsuspecting hand and turned away from my sisters.

"Savannah, what're you doing?" Sasha, my older sister by six minutes asked, lifting her sunglasses onto her forehead. "Just give the ball back."

"Oh, I'll give it back," I said, confidence raising my chin. Or was it the desire for payback?

"Savvy," said Talia, in her I'm-your-big-sister-and-I-know-what's-best voice. "Don't do anything stupid. The doctor warned you not to overdo it. Come back."

She grasped my arm, but I flung her hand away. "I had an aneurysm. *Had.* It got fixed. I'm not a freaking invalid!" Geez, my sisters drove me mad sometimes, especially Talia.

They treated me like a baby before the condition, but now it was ten times worse. They might as well have covered me in bubble wrap and attached me to a leash or something.

Talia crossed her arms and twisted her lips to one side as I approached the beach volleyballers. I stood at the corner of their makeshift court and shot a laser glare at Mr. I'm-So-Hot-It-Hurts. He stood at the ready, shifting his weight from one muscled leg to the other. Luckily, soccer wasn't my only forte. It'd been a while since I'd played volleyball, but I remembered how to do a mean serve. And I was determined that this would be my meanest.

My eyes pinned the location I was aiming for. I stepped back on my right foot and tossed the ball in the air, meeting it on its descent with the side of my thumb as my fingers clenched into a fist. Bam! The ball went over the net toward the incredibly gorgeous and incredibly infuriating guy, who lunged for it and missed. The ball left a kind of mini UFO crop circle in its wake on the sand. *Sucked in, hotshot.*

"Woo-hoo!" yelled a girl on my side of the net, approaching me with a high-five. "That was awesome. You're welcome to join us if you like."

I glanced toward Talia who tapped at her watch as if we were running late for something. The sun reflected off the silver and I squinted at the glare. Then I held up my hand and mouthed, "five minutes." I turned back to the girl. "Thanks, I'd love to."

I felt confident, powerful—*alive*. Hottie kept hitting the ball in my direction and only once did I miss. "I missed that on purpose," I said. "Thought I better let you have at least *one* point." He pretended to laugh, and I forced myself to look away from the silky ripple of a smile on his cheeks. I had to admit, he was pretty tough competition, but the thrill of opposing his every move sent a rush through my body I hadn't felt in a long time. Not since…

Oh. My. God.

I stopped. "Um, thanks guys, but I have to go now." I waved awkwardly to the group then rushed over to my sisters who'd actually been cheering on the sidelines.

"What's wrong, Savvy?" asked Talia, her brow furrowed.

"Nothing. But…I *saw* this." I gestured toward the volleyball match. "Everything that just happened, I've already seen it. Back in the hospital, right before I woke up." I placed my hands on my denim-clad hips and panted, catching my breath; from the exercise or the realization, I didn't know which. Silence followed as they were probably trying to process what I'd said.

Talia stepped closer to me, her height making me tilt my head up slightly. She nibbled on her bottom lip as though she was trying to work out a nice way of saying, "You're crazy, little sis." But she didn't. Quite the opposite, actually. "So did I. Only, I didn't see it, I *felt* it. The sand giving way under my feet, the warmth of the sun on my skin, the ice cream cones in my hands. Right before you woke up," she confessed.

My gaze locked on her intense blue eyes. I glanced at my other sisters who shifted awkwardly on the spot. At least if they thought I was crazy, my eldest sister would share the load with me. She'd felt this moment. I'd seen it. That was a fact, crazy or not.

Serena cleared her throat and scratched her cheek. "Me too," she whispered, stepping closer in alliance. "Moments before you woke, I heard you giggle, just like you did back there." She pointed to the ice cream van and squinted at the sun, crinkling her freckled nose. "I thought it was just a vivid memory at the time. I also heard the pop of the volleyball against everyone's hands, only I didn't realize what it was until now."

My heart rate kicked up a notch. And as though encouraged by our revelations, Sasha and Tamara looked at each other curiously and nodded.

"I could taste the ice cream," said Tamara, tucking a curly tendril of hair behind her ear, her round cheeks rosy under the heat of the sun.

"Wow, this is unbelievable," said Sasha. "I could smell the salty air and the sunscreen lotion." She shivered, despite the warm temperature.

The noise of the crowds and the splash of the waves subsided like we were the only people on the beach. My sisters' words floated through my mind, crisscrossing into a weave of realization. *The five senses.* One for each of us. "So what you're saying is, you *all* sensed this moment, in one way or another, right before I woke up?"

They nodded.

"Holy crap." I ran my fingers through my dark, bobbed hair until they met the hot sweat at the back of my neck. *How could this be possible?* "What were you doing at the time?" I asked, my mind searching for a plausible explanation.

Talia threaded her fingers together then stretched and wrung her hands. "We were thinking you might never wake up, and Serena started crying. She wouldn't let go of your hand," she explained.

"Then Talia put her arm around me," Serena added, glancing briefly at our sister.

"And we all joined hands around your bed," Talia said.

"Next thing I knew, I could feel sand under my feet and this wonderful, warm sensation came over me."

"Me too, just as I heard Savvy's laughter in my mind," Serena piped up. "And I felt kind of...I dunno..." She circled her hands as though trying to summon the sensation back into her body.

"Bubbly?" I asked, tilting my head a little.

Serena's jaw opened, and she gripped her smooth, dark ponytail, which hung over her shoulder. "Exactly! As though soda was inside me, bubbling up from my toes to my head."

"How the hell?" Tamara shook her head from side to side, her curls bouncing around her face. "Amazing."

"Do you think it'll ever happen again?" Sasha asked, crossing one foot over the other and placing a manicured hand on her hip.

I flashed a grin and held out my hands. "Only one way to find out."

CHAPTER 2

Nothing.

"Do you think we should close our eyes?" I glanced awkwardly at my sisters.

We closed our eyes.

Still nothing.

"Okay, what order were you in last time? Who was holding hands with who?" I pretended to be in a coma while my sisters shuffled around me.

"There, I'm sure that's how we were," said Tamara in her soft, reassuring voice.

We closed our eyes again, and waited...

Hmm.

"We weren't *exactly* like this," I said, sitting on the sand and maneuvering myself into a lying down position, as convincingly comatose as I could manage.

Nothing. Nada. Zilch.

"Oh, this is stupid!" Sasha got up and flicked sand off the back of her purple shorts. "It was obviously a one-off; let's forget it." Her cheeks flushed pink as she glanced around, probably worried that people on the beach would look at us like we'd escaped from an institution.

"You're probably right," Talia said. "Let's go back to the house; there's still heaps of unpacking to do." She flicked the sand off her behind too and smoothed down her dress. She turned to walk away, the others following suit.

"Savannah, you coming?" asked Serena with raised eyebrows.

With my butt still planted firmly on the sand, I hugged my knees to my chest. "We can't just forget about this. I mean, we saw the future. There must be a reason why it happened to us." I looked out at the sparkling, violet-blue ocean, hoping the waves would somehow wash ashore the secret of that day.

"I agree," Serena replied. "Nothing happens without some sort of explanation." She would probably start researching psychic phenomena as soon as we got home or brush up on the latest in neurology, possibly formulating a hypothesis and creating a PowerPoint presentation, all before dinner.

Talia stepped toward me. "Maybe there *is* an explanation, or maybe it was a fluke. Who knows?" She held out her hand. "But for now, let's head back home."

I paused a moment then grasped her hand, using it to help me up. "We have to try again." My eyes pleaded with my sister. "If it happened once it could happen again."

"Okay, let's make a pact to experiment with this...*ability*, every night before bed. Everyone agree?" Talia glanced around, her hand still in mine.

Heads nodded, anticipatory smiles formed, and footprints were left in the sand as we walked back to our new home. I didn't know what—if anything—would happen that night, but I couldn't wait to find out.

• • •

"I can't believe we live on a street called Roach Place. How gross." Sasha scrunched up her face as we rounded the corner into our new neighborhood.

"And number three, too. I don't know why, but it sounds like such an unlucky number," added Serena.

"Stop complaining, you two," I said. "Who cares what our street is called? We live five minutes from the beach, remember? I could live in a tent here and be happy." I marched on as they dawdled behind and glanced at number one, our neighbor. A man who looked to be in his midforties sat on a wrought-iron chair on his veranda. Our eyes connected. He looked away and stood, wiping his feet on the doormat, and then opened the whiny screen door that was in desperate need of some WD-40. "Looks like our new neighbor isn't the friendliest person on the planet."

"Who's complaining now?" said Serena, catching up to me.

"I'm just making an observation."

"Great," said Sasha. "We live at number three Roach Place and have a weirdo living next door. What's next?" She raised her palms. "Don't tell me, we'll have a spider infestation in the house or something."

"Ew! Don't talk about spiders." Talia shivered. So much for being the strong, fearless eldest sister.

"Most spiders are harmless," said Tamara, ever the animal lover. "If you don't bother them, they won't bother you."

"They bother me just by being visible." Talia shivered again and I chuckled. I wasn't exactly a fan of the eight-legged creatures either, but not much scared me anymore. Well, one thing did, but everything else was just stuff, little worries that didn't matter in the scheme of things. Having an aneurysm was one surefire way to put things into perspective.

We walked past the hedges separating our house from number one, and I snuck a glance back at the man's house. A flicker of his face was visible at the corner of the front window before the drapes ruffled and closed. So he was a weirdo *and* a Peeping Tom. Thank God my bedroom was on the other side of the house. If our other neighbors at number five weren't the friendly types either, our house would be trapped in one big weirdo sandwich. "We're back, Mom," Talia called out as we brushed sand off our bodies and stepped through the front door.

The clattering sound of pots and pans and sloshing water greeted us, muffling Mom's voice. "Hello darlings. I'm in the kitchen," she called out.

"Yeah, gathered that," I said, walking through to find her washing the dishes with more enthusiasm than anyone should have for such a chore. We had a dishwasher, but Mom always liked to give the dishes a "thorough cleaning" by hand whenever she was excited, stressed, or nervous about something. "What is it?"

"What's what?" she asked, lifting her shoulder to wipe away a clump of detergent from her rosy cheek.

"C'mon, Mom. Spill," I replied, giggling at the irony.

"That obvious, huh?" She smiled and put down the pan she'd been scrubbing. "I signed up for a part in a local play today."

"A play?"

"Yes. An amateur production called *Missing Inaction*. I don't know the whole story yet, I'll read the script tonight." She picked up the pan and resumed ridding it of every ounce of dirt, muck, and germs.

I exchanged glances with my sisters. Only a few days in a new town and Mom was embracing amateur theater? What would she do next, run off with the circus?

"Why? How did that happen? What role do you have?" Serena shot her questions in quick succession. She'd be a great game show host and an even better contestant.

"Yeah, how? Don't you have to audition or something first?" I asked.

"Already did," Mom replied with a smile that stretched high into her rounded cheeks. "I was at your new school getting your enrollments organized for next week, and I heard some commotion in the hall that adjoins the office." Mom gesticulated with her gloved hands and water splashed around the kitchen. Whenever she spoke, she seemed oblivious to things around her. "The receptionist told me it was a rehearsal for a play. So I wandered in and watched for a bit. The director seemed stressed, and he looked surprised when he saw me. One of the actors said I looked remarkably like some woman called Mona, who apparently was playing the lead role but broke her leg. So he asked if I'd ever done any acting before."

"But you haven't, have you?" Talia asked, wiping off a splash of water that had landed on her chin.

Mom's hands went to her hips. Water stains marred the sides of her top. "I'll have you know I was quite the accomplished actress in high school." She raised her chin.

"I might have continued later on in life but, well, I got busy with work, and, of course," she held a hand out to us, "thanks to the miracle of modern fertility treatment, I had twins, followed by the surprise of triplets around a year later. I had only planned for one more baby, but…good things come in threes, so they say! Anyway, I didn't exactly have time for anything that wouldn't help pay the bills."

"Well, sorry we got in the way of your Hollywood dreams, Mom," said Sasha with a hint of sarcasm.

"Oh, you girls." Mom wrapped a wet arm around Sasha, who grabbed a nearby tea towel for protection. "You never get in the way, you know that. But I thought I might as well take every opportunity in life now that we're starting fresh in Iris Harbor. Anyway, apparently I looked the part so he got me to read a few lines. It was fun; my character is a busy mother, so it was easy to get into the role." Mom winked. "Before I knew it, I'd been there an hour and a half and they made me the replacement for the lead role! The play's on in two months." She did a little jig.

"Is that enough time to rehearse?" I asked.

"It'll have to be," Mom said, returning to the pile of dishes. "And I expect you all to be there to witness my dazzling debut performance." She gave a flourished bow, splashing more water around, and I chuckled at having such a quirky mother.

Sasha, on the other hand, the self-conscious stunner of the family, covered her eyes with her fingers and shook her head. "Just don't embarrass us, Mom," she said, taking a stick of gum and popping it in her mouth before walking out of the kitchen.

Mom resumed her aquatic exploration, and I retreated to

my bedroom—well, mine, Serena's, and Sasha's bedroom—and opened a box of my belongings to unpack. Serena followed. Music blared through Sasha's iPod as she arranged makeup on the dressing table, even though she had her headphones in.

"Sasha, can you please turn that down?" Serena urged, raising her voice.

"What?" She pulled her earplugs out.

"I said, can you please turn that awful noise down?!" Serena covered her ears.

"Awful noise? That's no way to talk about a number-one hit single." She fiddled with the iPod.

"I wouldn't know. I don't keep track of all that stuff."

"You should, instead of listening to that geriatric classical stuff of yours."

Serena huffed. "It's well known that classical music improves learning, memory, and concentration. You should try it sometime." She gave her ponytail an indignant flick over her shoulder and resumed putting her book collection into the bookcase. Probably alphabetically.

"You calling me dumb?" Sasha planted her hands firmly on her hips and jutted her face forward.

"Geez, you girls! Stop fighting." I sighed and gave up on my unpacking then plonked myself on the bed and lay on my back. My gaze traced the decorative cornice framing the ceiling. "I can't stop thinking about today," I mused, not sure I'd even spoken loud enough for my sisters to hear.

Serena dropped a book and sat near my feet. "I can't either." She fiddled with the hem of her white T-shirt and twisted it into a knot.

"Or is it a certain *someone* you can't stop thinking about, huh?" Sasha flashed a cheeky pink-lipped grin.

"Hey!" I removed a pillow from behind my head and flung it at her. "Why would I want to think about that rude, conceited guy?"

"Ah," she placed her hands on her hips and tipped her head back a little. "So you *have* been thinking about him."

"No I haven't. I only thought about him now because you mentioned him."

"How did you know I was talking about *him*?"

"Who else? He was the one showing off and making himself known." I frowned and crossed my arms.

"Maybe he likes you," Serena said. "Don't guys act all rude and show-offy around girls they like?" She glanced at Sasha for confirmation.

I propped myself up on my elbows. "Or maybe he's just rude and show-offy *all* the time, more like it," I replied, even though something fluttered inside me, hoping I was wrong.

"I think Sasha's right. I think you *do* like him," Serena said with a smile.

"I do not!"

"Then why are your cheeks red?" asked Sasha. "Savannah has a thing for Volleyball Guy," she teased in a singsong voice, twirling her iPod cords around the device, and then placing it on the table.

I sat up and touched my hot cheeks. Damn. "I'm just hot from playing volleyball in the sun, that's all."

"Suuure," Sasha said in her husky voice, turning back to the dressing table and spritzing herself with perfume. Serena coughed and waved the scent away.

"Or maybe *you* like him, huh?" I countered. "Why are you putting on perfume now anyway? Do you plan to go out looking for Volleyball Guy or something?"

"As if. He's *so* not my type. Too casual and sporty and... sweaty. My man is going to be a successful, rich businessman. You wait and see. I'll be back in the city as soon as I'm out of school, and we'll live in a gorgeous apartment together. I'm not settling for some small town guy who'd rather work on his tan than his bank balance." She gave herself another spritz. If she kept that up, we'd soon need oxygen masks. And if there *was* a successful, rich businessman out there for her, I bet he could smell her perfume from all the way in the city.

Sasha was so idealistic. Did she really think she'd score a hotshot tycoon and live a life of glamour like some silver-spooned heir? Life didn't work that way, but no matter what happened, Sasha preferred to live in her safe little bubble of "everything's perfect" land.

I flopped onto my back and exhaled deeply. "So anyway. After dinner, yeah? We'll...you know...try again?"

Serena nodded. "Can't wait. What if something happens again? Do you think it will?" She gripped the hem of her T-shirt again.

"Doubt it." Sasha removed the elastic from her ponytail and swished her hair around her shoulders.

She could be right, but something told me our vision at the hospital wasn't meant to be our one and only.

• • •

"You ready?" Talia asked, her blue eyes unblinking.

We nodded, entwining our hands in each other's. Serena's were sweaty; she always got nervous easily. What if we did see something? Something important, even? Well, *I'd* see it, but if things played out as they did before, then each of my sisters would "see" it with only one of the five senses. It was like we were one body, needing each other to fully comprehend what was going on. I was the eyes, Serena the ears, Sasha the nose, Tamara the tongue, and Talia the hands. Bizarre!

My heart pounded as we closed our eyes and waited. I tightened my grip on Serena and Tamara's hands, if only to steady Serena's trembling.

"This is stupid," said Sasha, sighing. "Nothing's happening."

A sudden jolt sharpened my posture, and a sense of déjà vu washed through my mind. My feet tingled, and a familiar sensation rose from my toes to my head, a sensation that could only be described as…bubbly.

CHAPTER 3

Light danced and swirled behind my closed eyes until the array of muted colors formed an image. A masculine hand reached out to turn a doorknob, as though it was my hand and I was the one opening the door. I couldn't feel anything, no smooth metal against my hand or the lightness of the door giving way as I pulled it open. I could only see it happening in front of me. Then blackness. Then something else. *What is that?* My mind's eye focused on something glossy. Was it the ocean at night? No, something plastic? Oh, it's just a garbage bag tied in a knot. *Why am I seeing this?*

Thoughts raced through my mind as I made sense of what I was seeing. Maybe it was my imagination playing tricks on me, random images popping up for no reason. But I'd distinctly felt that same bubbly sensation I'd had in the hospital.

"Ew!"

My eyes snapped open at Sasha's exclamation, and we broke away from each other's grasp. "What?" I asked.

"Yuck. I just got a whiff of something off, like old meat and food scraps. Like I'd stuck my head inside a garbage can."

"You did?" My eyes widened. "I saw a bag of garbage. It was dark, though, so I didn't know what it was at first, but it was definitely a garbage bag packed to the brim." I eyed each of my sisters, waiting for their responses.

"All I heard was footsteps and some sort of crinkling sound, then a dull slap of something," said Serena. Her eyes opened wider and she held up her finger. "Oh! Could it have been the lid of a garbage can?"

I shrugged, but Serena seemed sure she'd come to the correct conclusion. This was getting interesting. Even though rotting meat and garbage weren't exactly a riveting topic of discussion, we'd all tuned into the same thing. "Tamara? Talia?"

Tamara cleared her throat. "I don't know if it was just the aftertaste of the sausages we had for dinner, but I tasted meat, maybe steak. It wasn't off though, phew! And after that, something minty. A Tic Tac or Mentos? Did I imagine it?" She licked her lips as though trying to return to the sensation. Or maybe it had made her hungry. It didn't take much to boost Tamara's voracious appetite.

Talia shook her head. "I definitely felt something. The plastic bag in my hand, the heavy weight of it, and then the release as I dumped it," she said. "Oh, and before that, cold metal against my hand, like a doorknob." She looked at her palm and gave it a rub; the thin silver ring on her middle finger glinting under the ceiling light.

"Whoa." I ran my fingers through my hair. "I *saw* the doorknob, only it was a male hand touching it, not mine."

"Too weird," said Tamara.

"Too stupid," said Sasha. "And gross. Why did I have to luck out and get stuck with the crappy smells?"

Serena giggled.

"It's not stupid," I said. "It worked. We had a vision again. Something's definitely happening to all of us."

"But seriously, a bag of garbage? What's so exciting about that?" Sasha crossed her arms and her bangles jingled.

"Maybe we're just getting warmed up," Talia suggested. "Should we try again?"

We joined hands and closed our eyes. I prepared myself to once again feel the bubbly sensation.

The door flung open. "What are you girls up to?" Mom asked.

We dropped our hands and tried to act normal. "Nothing, just mucking around," I said, rubbing the back of my neck.

"Yeah," agreed Sasha, sitting on her bed and grabbing a magazine.

"Well, it's good to see you all wanting to spend time together. There's a good movie about to start on TV, do you want to watch it with me?"

The last thing I wanted was to try to focus on something else when what was happening to us was way more interesting. "No, we're all right, aren't we girls?" I glanced at my sisters.

They nodded. "Yep, we're just having some girl time, and Savvy's telling us about the boy she likes."

"I am not, Sasha!" I shot her a warning glare.

"Ooh, who is he?" asked Mom.

"No one. There is no guy. Sasha's just playing games. You go ahead and watch the movie, Mom."

Mom pouted. "All right then, I know when I'm not

wanted." She smiled in resignation and closed the door.

I added an extra glare in Sasha's direction for good measure, and she stood up and we held hands again.

Bubbles, bubbles, come to Mama...

Nothing. Only blackness.

"Looks like the revolting garbage is all we're seeing for now guys," said Talia, pulling away and leaning her tall, slim frame against the wall.

"But that can't be all. What does it mean?" Serena asked.

"That we'll each have to take turns putting out the garbage like we do anyway? Big whoop." Sasha slumped on the edge of her bed.

"Do you think the garbage is literal or metaphorical?" Serena continued. "Is it *really* garbage, or is it symbolic of throwing away our old life and starting fresh?"

"Nothin' fresh about what I smelled!" Sasha chuckled and Tamara snorted.

Serena ignored her, too deep in thought. She furrowed her brow, and I could almost see her brain working, running through the possibilities. Her mind probably had its own spreadsheet with columns and categories. It must be exhausting living in her head. Sometimes I've heard her whispering to herself late at night when she thought I was asleep. I knew it was just her way of processing the day in order to wind down and sleep, to make sense of things and plan for the day ahead. Occasionally she'd jot things down on a notepad beside her bed. As for me, the events of the day always replayed through my mind like a movie, and sometimes I'd even imagine things that hadn't happened, like a waking dream. Just my overactive imagination. But now, now I'd think twice about any picture that popped into my mind. What if all those random images I'd become used to seeing were not my imagination, but visions? Visions of things happening somewhere else in the world, or even visions of things that were *going* to happen?

"I have an idea." Tamara rubbed her hands together the way she often did when it was time for dessert. In fact, I almost thought she was about to suggest we eat dessert and leave further analysis of our vision until tomorrow. "Let's keep a journal, write down everything we see. Or taste or smell or whatever." Tamara looked around the room. "Is there a notebook we can use?"

"Here." Serena sat on her bed and pulled open her bedside drawer, which was neatly organized. "Nothing written in this one yet." She opened it, grabbed a pen, and wrote the date at the top of the first page. "What should we call it?"

"Call what?"

"The journal. Should we give it a name like *Visions* or something?"

"Don't be silly. If anyone finds it they'll cart us off to a psych ward," said Sasha, reaching into her pocket and popping some gum into her mouth.

Tamara tapped the notebook with her finger. "Just write the date and what we sense, that's all we need."

Serena wrote each of our names, and, next to them, what we all sensed. I walked over to the window and held the drapes aside. "Wow, guys, we predicted that it was garbage night. How exciting," I said flatly, eyeing the garbage cans lining the cul-de-sac of Roach Place that we now called home. Mom had already put ours out. A lone street light cast a glare of brightness at the beginning of the street. The rest of Roach Place faded into muted darkness with eerie shadows floating across the ground as trees swayed gently in the night breeze.

"Forget about the garbage," Serena said. "Maybe it'll make sense later. We'll put every detail in this journal from now on and keep reading back over it. Something might click down the road." Serena was in her element with pen and notebook in hand; if she didn't have her head stuck in a book, she was either writing or watching some science documentary on YouTube. Unlike Sasha who preferred to watch music videos or addictive soapies. It was hard to believe those two were related, let alone shared the same womb for nine months, along with me.

"So, how do you think we got this *ability*?" asked Tamara, sitting cross-legged on Sasha's bed, her baggy T-shirt looking more like a dress. "I wonder if it had something to do with your coma, Savvy. Maybe we all picked up on some weird brain thing that was happening to you." She circled a hand next to her head.

"That reminds me." Serena stood, as though a surge of electricity sparked a boost in energy, and she couldn't possibly remain seated. "It was about a month before you woke up, and I was pestering the doctor to explain things to me: How the coma happened. What it meant. What was going on inside your brain at the time, and all that." She paced the room. "He talked about the different brain waves people have, and I remembered learning a bit about them in school. He mentioned something about *delta* brain waves and that they only occur during deep sleep or comas. He said maybe you just needed extra 'delta time' to heal. I think it was his way of making things sound better, when really…he didn't know whether you'd wake up or not." My sister looked at me with glossy eyes. "It could have something to do with that. Your brain waves might have changed somehow." She opened up our laptop—ours, because Mom couldn't afford five for all of us and we hadn't received our school laptops yet—and typed into Google.

"What are you doing?" I asked.

"Shh." Her dainty fingers tapped away quickly on the keyboard, and she scrolled through the search results on the screen, clicking back and forth on a few links.

Sasha sighed. "I don't want a science lesson; school doesn't start for a few more days." She leaned back on the bed and flipped through her magazine.

"Hang on, what's this?" Serena clicked on a webpage. "Psychic ability and brain waves. Ooh, look!" She pointed and we peered at the screen. "It says that they hooked up some alleged psychics to EEGs—that's a type of test to measure brain activity—and some were found to be experiencing delta waves while in the psychic state. Normally the person needs to be asleep for that to happen, but these psychics were fully awake and conscious." Serena's eyes were wide, and her pale skin held a faint glow. She looked the same way Tamara looked when sitting down to eat her favorite dessert.

"So what you're saying is, they had these…delta wave thingies while awake, when in reality that's impossible?" asked Talia.

"I guess so. Maybe during delta waves we tap into some other consciousness or intuition, but we don't usually remember anything because we've been asleep; but if you're awake, then…" She held her hand toward the screen.

"You might be able to recall what you experienced," Talia reasoned and Serena nodded.

"But how do we even know this website is for real? It could be some hoax," said Sasha.

"Maybe or maybe not. Look, the researcher is a doctor."

"Yeah, anyone could put an MD next to their name on a website." Yet Sasha seemed convinced of the validity of the information in her glossy magazine.

"Stop being so skeptical, Sasha. You experienced the vision just like we did. There has to be an explanation." Serena continued reading. "It's possible that Savvy was experiencing delta waves in her coma, and when we all gathered around her, it could have triggered something in all of us." Serena's eyes lit up like she'd just invented electricity.

"So somehow, for some reason, we could be experiencing delta waves while awake, during these *episodes* of ours?" Talia asked. She needed an explanation just as much as Serena, but I had a feeling it was more to feel in control than to understand the underlying mechanism. Me, I just wanted to know what the significance of it all was. Why us? What would happen next? And what should we do about it?"

"Yes, that could be what's happening," replied Serena. "I don't know how it's possible, but there's a lot science doesn't know yet. The fact that we're sisters—triplets and twins at that—could have enhanced our connection to Savvy on some other level and somehow caused her brain waves to impact ours. It could have created a compound effect of enhanced sensory awareness as though we're all sharing one highly sensitive brain."

I shook my head in awe of my sister. She was most certainly Einstein reincarnated.

"What do we do then? Go to the hospital and ask them to hook us all up to EEGs while we hold hands and chant?"

Sasha chuckled.

"Yeah, right," Tamara replied. "We don't have to get tested for anything. Serena's just trying to make sense of what's happening to us, and it sounds pretty cool to me." She placed her hand on Serena's shoulder.

Could my coma really have triggered some deep, hidden ability? Did we have this all along and it simply needed a near-death situation to bring it into reality?" A smile tickled my cheeks. "If this is true, then maybe we're like *Delta Sisters* or something."

"That sounds like a pop group to me," said Serena. "I prefer *Delta Girls*. That sounds better." She gave a firm nod and a strand of dark hair came loose from her ponytail.

"Yeah, I like that." Talia nodded. A name, a label would probably make her feel more secure in what was happening to us. The way a patient seeks a diagnosis to make sense of their symptoms. It may not change anything, but it gives a sense of certainty to the uncertain.

We all smiled, even Sasha. "That *does* sound pretty cool," she said.

Whether giving our ability or ourselves a name would help us understand this phenomenon though, I had no idea; but having something concrete to start with, to make it real, felt good.

The words scrolled across the screen of my mind. My mouth gaped. "Hey, take out the c, a, and r from our surname and you have the word *delta*," I said. "How weird is that?"

"Oh yeah!" Tamara said. "Meant to be."

My grin widened. To others we would always be the Delcarta sisters. But to us, we were now officially the *Delta Girls*.

• • •

It wasn't like I—*we*—had a mega superpower or anything, but my body buzzed knowing it could do something out of the ordinary. It was a nice change to feeling tired, achy, scared, and weak like I had been after waking from my coma. My muscles were gradually getting their strength back after being sedentary for so long, and my body wanted to catch up on missed time and make the most of being alive; really feel that pulsing force of blood through my veins— go running, swim naked even, and spin around till I was dizzy. And usually late at night when everyone was asleep. I couldn't switch my mind off, both from the excitement at having had another vision, and the general feeling of getting better with each passing day.

Darkness surrounded me in the room, apart from a small sliver of moonlight creeping through the side of the drapes above my bed. Mom had given me the window bed under the assumption that being the night owl in the family, the morning sun shining on my face would help me wake each day in time for school. But now, that same window only kept me awake. I'd have to get an eye mask.

A slight click diverted my attention outside, and I sat up and peered through the gap in the drapes. Across the road, someone walked out of his front door. He stepped off the porch and walked to the curb where the moon shone on his skin—his bare-chested skin that was practically cling-wrapped around firm muscles. The shadows slid aside to reveal a face that, although a little distant, was unmistakably the same face I'd glared at earlier in the day. Volleyball Guy.

Oh my God. *He lives across the road?* Oh man, I'd never

hear the end of it from my sisters. Why would they even think I liked him? He was plain rude and a complete tool. So his physique was impressive, but that didn't mean a thing.

I closed the gap in the drapes a tad, but kept my eyes fixed on him. Then déjà vu hit me right when he lifted his arm and flung a heavy garbage bag in an arc across his body and into the garbage can that sat in waiting on the curbside. I saw it, we all saw it, or *sensed* it. So it may not have been the most exciting premonition of the century, but we were only—as Talia suggested—warming up with our ability. The hand I'd seen opening the doorknob was his. The garbage bag—his. And as he walked back inside his house and closed the door, I smiled as a realization eased into my consciousness: somehow, I'd gotten inside his head—his perception—and he had absolutely no idea.

This gift could turn out to be a *whole* lot of fun.

I was about to close the drapes and settle in under the sheets when something to the right caught my eye. Movement. In a flash, a hooded figure scurried away, and I couldn't be sure, but it looked like he'd come from the side of our house, somewhere near the carport. He disappeared beyond the hedges between number one and us. I couldn't see past them as the road sloped downward from there. Was it our neighbor? I tiptoed out of the bedroom and into the living room, and then pulled the drapes aside on the window beside the fireplace. His lights weren't on, but he could have slipped back inside after walking around the hedge. *Should I wake my sisters? My Mom?* I tiptoed back to the room and glanced at Sasha's and Serena's beds where they lay completely out of it. Mom had no doubt fallen asleep in front of the TV and dragged herself off to bed after a while.

I didn't want to disturb them. Maybe he hadn't come from the side of our house; maybe he was looking for a lost cat or something, or taking a shortcut home through the back of our property. It was probably nothing. Surely if it was something important we would have seen it in our vision— wouldn't we?

CHAPTER 4

"Bye, girls, have a good first day at school!" Mom called out as we stepped outside, the sun blazing down and creating an instant film of sweat under my shirt.

"I'm sure we will," I said with overt and fake enthusiasm, sliding sunglasses over my eyes. Everything seemed brighter than usual. "Enjoy your first day at work, Mom." I waved, and her sandy, curly hair bounced as she turned back inside.

Mom had scored a massage therapist position at a snazzy holistic day spa on the main street in town. She used to work from home when us kids were young, and also did the odd bit of counseling, but now she wanted the freedom of having a separate workplace. I didn't know how much they were paying her, but it couldn't be a huge amount. If it wasn't for Grandma Delcarta's money getting wired to us regularly, we'd probably be homeless. Raising five kids on her own had not been an easy thing for Mom since Dad… well, since that difficult time. And despite her overbearing motherly ways, she was a good mom, especially during my illness. I don't know what I would have done without her. I took a deep breath and tried to push the past from my mind.

"Well, well, well, if it isn't Volleyball Girl." I turned my head toward the voice. *Well, well, well, if it isn't Volleyball Guy.* He sat atop a bike, swerving left and right to keep it to a slow ride alongside us as we walked down the road.

"My name is Savannah, not Volleyball Girl." Not that it would stop me from calling *him* Volleyball Guy.

He jabbed his foot into the ground to regain balance. "Looks like we're neighbors."

"Looks that way." I kept my eyes straight ahead, and he didn't make any effort to move faster. His bag hung easily on his back as though it wasn't even putting any weight on him, and his eyes were shielded by black sunglasses, like mine.

"So why did you run off midmatch the other day? Couldn't handle the pressure?" One corner of his mouth lifted slightly.

I glared in his direction, disappointed he wouldn't be able to see it on account of my sunglasses. But I didn't want to take them off; then it would look like I *wanted* to speak to him. "The only pressure I was aware of was on *you.*" There. *I'll show him who's boss.* "I had to be somewhere; that's why I left."

"Yeah," Talia chimed in, moving closer to me. "We had a…thing, to get to, didn't we?" Her gaze recruited the support of my other sisters who nodded, and Sasha removed her iPod earplugs.

"Oh, sure," he replied with a smirk.

I wondered what his reaction would be if I simply said: "Actually, I stopped playing because I realized I'd had a psychic vision about that very same volleyball match, and

I ran off to tell my sisters who revealed that they too had a psychic episode, and so we all held hands and closed our eyes and tried to make it happen again." At least if I'd had the guts to say that he might have cycled off and left us alone, but the words stayed in my mind.

"Just so you know," he continued, "your team lost."

"Boohoo. I'm shattered," I replied, my gaze straight ahead.

"I bet they would have won if Savvy had stayed." Sasha raised her chin and scowled at Volleyball Guy, and I grinned.

"Savvy, huh? I wonder how *savvy* you really are," he teased. "I'd like to see if you can beat us at another match. If you're up for it, that is?" A one-sided grin dimpled his bronze cheek.

"Of course I'm up for it," I said, before even thinking whether I was. Mentally, yes, but physically? I gulped. Talia eyed me with concern as if to say, "Remember what the doctor said." But in reality they probably only said those things to protect themselves from getting sued. Of course I needed time to get back to my old self, but I was almost there. What I lacked in physical strength and endurance, I could make up for in sheer determination.

"Ten a.m. this Saturday at the beach. See you there, Volleyball Girl." I'm sure behind those sunglasses he winked as he lifted his firm butt off the bike seat and pushed his feet on the pedals to pick up speed. His calf muscles bulged, and in a flash he rode around the corner we were headed for and disappeared. *Don't tell me we go to the same school?* Oh joy.

• • •

"Hey, Sis," I said as Serena and I crossed paths with Tamara in the humid and stuffy school hallway. "How's school for you?"

"Meh," she said, shrugging. "Although I did find out Volleyball Guy's name; he's in a couple of my classes. Riley Pearce."

"Why should I care?"

"Well, now we can stop calling him Volleyball Guy." She took a sip from her water bottle.

"That's on the assumption that we'll be talking about him again, and I don't see why we'd want to do that."

"Geez, touchy! Sorry, I won't mention him anymore. At least not until we get home, how about that?" She grinned.

I shook my head. "You and Sasha are as bad as each other."

Tamara took another sip of water. "This water tastes a bit sour. Must be the heat or something." She shrugged and gulped more down anyway, and then looked in the direction we were headed. "What subject have you got now?"

"Science," Serena said with a level of enthusiasm that should only be reserved for lunchtime and home time.

"Yeah," I said. "Serena and I are in the same class, thank God. She can help me with my homework." I winked at my sister and she rolled her eyes.

"Do you think we should ask the science teacher about delta brain waves?" she asked.

"What? No!" I said.

"I don't mean tell him about what happened to us, just casually ask if he's heard of any cases of delta waves being predominant while awake." She said it like it was as simple as asking the teacher what time class finished.

"It's our first day, I think we should just let him do his job and not attract attention to ourselves."

"She's right, Serena," said Tamara. "One step at a time." She took a mint from her bag and popped it in her mouth as she walked off.

Two minutes later, Serena and I entered Science Lab Three. Serena headed for the front. "Hey," I whispered. "Let's sit in the middle, not up front like a couple of know-it-alls." She looked at me as if to say, "But I *am* a know-it-all," then sighed and sat at a desk in the middle. There were three chairs to each desk, and I wanted my sister with me so she could take charge of any practical experiments. At least Volleyball Guy—*Riley*—wasn't in my year and wouldn't be sharing any classes with me.

A tall girl with light brown hair gathered in a scrunchie at the nape of her neck sat next to me. I gave her a brief smile. Hers was briefer, and she diverted her gaze quickly from mine. If Sasha was there I could imagine her whispering into my ear, "Scrunchies? I mean, *seriously?*" and shaking her head in disapproval. My own hair wasn't long enough for a scrunchie or any sort of hair elastic. I'd had it cut short a few months back as I knew they'd be shaving some of it off for the operation. It had grown back now and was the same length as the rest, though I was still in the habit of styling my hair in a sweeping arc across my head.

The teacher was busy writing stuff on the whiteboard as we got our books and pens ready. Serena wrote the date at the top of her notebook page, just like she'd done with our "visions" journal, but this time it would be filled with boring scientific facts. Okay, so I was mildly interested in what had happened to me, but more than that, I was glad to see the back of that hospital. Any talk of the human body brought it all back, and it was something I'd rather not think about anymore. Luckily, by the looks of what the teacher was writing on the board, we'd be learning something to do with space and black holes today. Riveting. I just wanted to hurry and grow up, finish school, and start my real life. Move my body, have fun, and make the most of life, not be stuck in a classroom.

I opened my notebook and sighed, tapping the pen against the paper. "Shh," Serena whispered, flicking me on the arm.

The girl next to me also wrote the date at the top of her notebook, and then laid out a ruler, pencil, eraser, and sharpener neatly near the edge of the desk. I mean, *really* neatly. She even adjusted them a few times as though making sure they were of equal distance apart. Her short fingernails were painted in different colors. Not random, opposite colors, but similar variations of pink, red, and orange; each color blended into the next, sort of like flames. "Your nails look good," I remarked.

She looked at her hands and spread her fingers apart. "I know. The graduation of color is pleasing to the eye," was all she said. I was going to introduce myself, but the teacher, a thinnish man in an unassuming gray shirt and darker gray trousers, placed his marker on the edge of the whiteboard and slowly turned around.

"Welcome, students. For those who don't know me, I'm Mr. Jenkins."

My breath halted in my chest. *No way!* My head swiveled to the left and Serena's mouth was slightly gaping too. Our neighbor was our teacher? Oh man, that was it, we had to move. Number three Roach Place next door to a weirdo science teacher and across the road from an irritating smart-mouthed annoyingly good-looking jerk. Just great.

"Still want to ask him about delta waves?" I whispered to Serena, and she shushed me again.

I shifted uncomfortably in my seat as Mr. Jenkins began the roll call in a monotone voice that I thought could be a possible solution to my insomnia, and I tried to remember the names of as many students as I could.

"Savannah Delcarta?"

"Here." I raised my hand feebly, and he glanced up from his list, his eyes fixing on mine for a moment or two longer than was comfortable. He recognized me.

He shifted his gaze to my sister. "And you must be Serena Delcarta?"

"Yes, sir." She nodded, and everybody turned their heads to look at us.

I felt like saying "What? So we're sisters, big deal!" At least Serena, Sasha, and I weren't identical. Tamara and Talia weren't either. I'd feel for poor Mom if we were; she'd probably get us all confused, and for all I knew I could really be Serena and Serena could be me or what she thought was me. My mind drifted as I pondered whether that had actually happened to anyone in real life—if any twins or triplets had been mixed up as infants and ended up unknowingly becoming the other sibling. I held back a chuckle, and when I shook my distracted thoughts away, I realized I'd missed Mr. Jenkins' instructions and had to check Serena's textbook to see what page to read.

The words blurred under my gaze, and I forced myself to focus; but the letters were fuzzy, and they hovered and floated like bubbles. I squeezed my eyes shut and reopened them, but that only made things worse. So I rubbed my eyes and blinked a few times. The words on the page were like pins poking into my eyes, and I couldn't read anymore. I glanced to the girl next to me whose name I'd failed to discover due to my daydreaming, and who was using her ruler to speed-read, sliding it down the page with her bright fingernails that were no longer "pleasing to the eye." I looked around the lab, tension clenching my shoulders. Fluorescent lighting rods beamed down from above like spotlights; the sun shone through windows and reflected sharply off the stainless steel sinks, burning my eyes. The faces of the students all looked the same. *What's going on?* My heart pounded as a scary thought entered my mind like an unwelcome visitor. *What if my aneurysm was back?* What if the surgery had been a waste of time and the little bastard had decided to rear its ugly head again? I clamped my eyes shut and covered them with my trembling hands.

"Miss Delcarta, is something wrong?" Mr. Jenkins asked, narrowing his eyes.

I opened my eyes and could barely make out his face. *Oh God.* I turned to Serena. Her blurry face was scrunched up, and she was rubbing her ears like there was a rock band playing at a thousand decibels next door. We exchanged glances of confusion, and although my eyes burned and stung and I wanted to stick my head in a bucket of ice cold water, I took comfort in the assumption that it probably wasn't another aneurysm, as Serena seemed just as distressed as me. *Serena—she hears things. Me—I see things. Ears. Eyes. They both hurt.*

My chair screeched as I stood. "I have a bad headache,

sir. I need to go...take something."

Before he could respond, I dashed from the classroom, faintly hearing Serena's voice saying, "I'll go see if she's okay."

I pushed open the door to the girls' bathroom and splashed water on my face. "What's happening?" I asked. "My eyes are burning!" I looked in the mirror but they weren't red.

"I don't know; my ears are stinging and everything seems so loud!" Serena whispered, and then jumped as the bathroom door flung open and Sasha barged in, rummaging through her bag and extracting a can of body spray.

"Huh? What are you two doing here?" she asked.

"What are *you* doing here?" I squinted.

"There was a bad smell in my English classroom, and I had to get out of there; but no one else could smell it." She sprayed the cheap perfume all over her body. "I can't get rid of it! Smells like burnt toast."

"I think we're having some sort of enhanced sensory disturbance," said Serena, still rubbing her ears, her hair coming loose from the thin elastic of her ponytail.

Not only did my eyes burn, but they darted here, there, and everywhere, taking in every little detail of my surroundings. A visual stampede of colors, shapes, lines, textures, patterns, and light shoved themselves at my eyes. My breath quickened, and I feared I might have a panic attack.

The door swung open and Tamara and Talia burst in with confused expressions on their faces. Tamara turned on a tap, bent toward it, and drank from it, then spat out the water. "I can't get rid of this disgusting burnt taste." She wiped her mouth and stuck out her tongue.

Talia ran her hands under cold water. "My hands are so

hot! What's going on?"

"Quick, let's join hands!" I said. "Maybe it's trying to get a vision to us." I held my hands out, not knowing what I meant by "it," just wanting whatever it was to stop.

As I squeezed my eyes shut, bubbles rose inside me and my breath slowed as the painful light behind my eyes eased into an image of a match being lit. Bright orange flickered and curled and every detail was clear. The tiny flame from the match grew into one enormous flame, and then hundreds of flames, dancing and teasing and feeding off each other. An explosion burst into my view and I flinched, yellowy flames curling into a cloud-shaped ball, smoke drifting toward the sky. My breathing quickened again, not from pain, but from the sight. Geez, talk about intense! Not what I was expecting after the anticlimax of our previous garbage can vision. We hadn't experienced another one since then. Until now. The image moved aside like in a slideshow, and I saw a bottle roll along the ground, and—

"What are you girls all doing in here? Get back to class, please!"

I jumped, opened my eyes, and all I could see now was the angry face of a female teacher. The wiry frizz of her gray hair held a sense of irritation to match her voice.

"Well, c'mon! You can chat and discuss boys at lunchtime, girls."

I clamped my lips together in a straight line. *She has no freaking idea.*

"Sorry, Miss, we were just... um," Talia began.

"Savannah had a bad headache, and my sisters and I were checking if she was okay, that's all," Serena said.

"Yeah. I had an operation a few months ago so they

were just worried." I wasn't one for seeking out sympathy, but hey, if this could help us avoid getting detention, I might as well use it.

"Oh. And are you feeling better now? Do you need me to call your parents?"

I resisted the urge to correct the term to *parent*. Something else she had no freaking idea about. "No. I'm fine." The pain had gone. The lighting was normal.

"Very well, back to class then." The teacher stood with her hand holding the door open until we filtered out.

Damn, we didn't get to finish and discuss what we'd sensed. Although, it was so intense I didn't know if I wanted to.

• • •

At dinner that night, Mom fidgeted, pushing her food around the plate and continually asking us if we wanted more rice, more juice, or more bread.

"Do you need to go wash the dishes, Mom?" I teased, curious about what was on her mind now.

"Oh yes, I must give them a good hand wash after dinner. Definitely." She fiddled with her wedding ring. She still wore it after all those years. My guess was that if she removed it, she'd remove whatever hope was left too.

I put my knife and fork down. "Okay, what's on your mind? Are you nervous about the play?" I asked.

"What? The play? No, I mean a little. But…" She drew a deep breath and smiled. "I got a phone call today."

"What sort of phone call?"

She cleared her throat. "Remember how I had to take

the car to the mechanic last week when it kept stalling for some reason? Well, the mechanic, Wayne Rickers, called me when I got home from work today and…" Mom giggled. "He asked me out!"

I was glad I'd already swallowed my bite of chicken or I might have choked. "You mean on a date?"

"Yes! Isn't that exciting?" Her hands disappeared under the table, as though trying to hide the fact from her wedding ring.

My mom going on a date? "But—"

"I know, I know, it feels weird, right?" Mom's hands reappeared, and she leaned her elbows on the table; her excessive curls flung forward in front of her shoulders. "But, it's been nine years since your father…disappeared, and I thought it was about time I made an effort to move on." Mom raised her shiny eyes to the ceiling as though seeking Dad's permission from somewhere in the ether, even though we had no idea whether he was dead or alive. After nine years—I didn't hold out much hope; but as long as we didn't know for sure, there was still a chance he could find us and walk through that door with his wide smile and outstretched arms, his wavy hair flopping over his eyes, and his love for all of us plain to see. A ripple of sadness rolled through me and I bowed my head.

"I know this might be a bit of a shock to you, but it's just a simple date. Dinner and a movie, that's all. You know that no one will ever take your father's place." Mom grasped Talia's and Tamara's hands, as they were seated next to her.

Serena sniffled and pushed her chair back. "I'm sorry. I'm pleased for you, Mom, it's just…" Tears threatened at the brim of her eyelids, and she dashed out of the dining room.

"I'll go," I said, standing. "And, Mom, it *is* about time you got out there. I'm happy for you." I forced a smile and followed Serena to the bedroom.

"It was bound to happen sooner or later," I said, wrapping my arms around my sister, who in that moment seemed even shorter and more petite than me.

"I know," she sobbed. "It just makes everything seem so final, that's all."

"I know." I tightened my jaw to stop my bottom lip from quivering.

"What if he's still out there? What if he comes back?" She buried her face in my shoulder and moisture seeped through my shirt.

I hated to say it, to even think it, but if he hadn't come back by now, I doubted he ever would. He hadn't walked out on us, there was no way. He and Mom were happy together; *we* were happy together. I knew in my heart that something bad had happened, and Mom knew it too. She wouldn't tell me what she'd spoken to the police about back then; I was too young—we all were. But there was no doubt in my mind that Dad had met with foul play. The police had given up after a while when all leads had failed, and he'd never been found.

I held my sister until she calmed down, and after my other sisters had finished dinner and Mom had vigorously washed the dishes herself—practically needing to swim out of the kitchen—we gathered in my bedroom.

"We still have to write down what happened today in our journal." Serena took the notepad from her bedside table. It hit me then that by keeping her mind busy with other things, she could distract herself from the memory of Dad's disappearance. And by striving to understand anything and everything about the universe, she was temporarily filling that gap inside—that need to know and understand what happened. It wasn't the same as knowing the real truth about Dad, but it kept her going. We all dealt with what happened in our own way, and that was hers.

I placed a supportive hand on Serena's back as she filled in the date and our names, and then wrote what she'd heard during the vision: a loud bang, like an explosion, and the roar and rumble of a fire. Her experience was like the soundtrack to the movie I'd seen in my mind. Sasha had, of course, experienced a burnt smell, and, in addition, the scent of alcohol.

"I saw a bottle rolling along the ground," I added to my statement.

"I could taste alcohol, but it was really strong and awful," said Tamara, scrunching her face.

"When have you had alcohol, anyway?" Sasha asked.

"At New Year's Eve a year ago, remember? We snuck some from the wine casket in the hall when Mom's friends weren't looking?"

"I didn't have any." Sasha pouted.

"You were only fifteen, I wouldn't let you," said Talia. "It was gross anyway. So, all I could feel in the vision was the heat on my hands and my face."

Serena scribbled down the details. "A fire. What are we supposed to do with this information? Do you think we're safe here? What if there's going to be a fire? Maybe we should tell Mom."

"Don't be silly, Serena. We can't tell Mom; she might send us all to the doctor," Sasha said. "Anyway, I don't see how we'd have a fire here. It's still summer and we don't have a working fireplace. We haven't even unpacked the box with all the candles."

"Even so, let's steer clear of anything that could be a risk," Talia instructed, looking concerned. "What about the oven? It might be a bit old. Maybe I should casually tell Mom to get it checked out and make sure it's still in good working order."

"Great idea." Serena nodded.

"I'll ask her. After all, I *am* the budding chef in the family." Tamara smiled and swayed from side to side. "It won't sound weird coming from me."

"True. Okay, ask her tomorrow before dinner," said Talia, her face softening a little from its usual creased and worried appearance. She was a bit like me, needed to do something practical to deal with things.

"So, the first vision we had came true, what—three months later?" Serena wrote it down. "But the second vision, the one about the garbage, nothing happened with that, did it?" She glanced around.

I cleared my throat. "Um, actually, I might have forgotten to mention something." All eyes looked at me. I didn't think it was important enough to tell them before, and if I'd brought up Riley again they'd have more reason to tease me. "After you'd all gone to sleep that night, I looked out my window and saw Riley come out of his house across the road. He was carrying a bag of garbage, and he dumped it in his can. That's all. No biggie." I shrugged.

"Yes it is," said Serena, shooting up to standing. "It still means that something we saw came true, even if it was only a little thing. We need to document *everything* that happens in case there's a pattern of some kind. And we can't keep any secrets, okay?"

"Okay, fair enough," I replied.

"That's not exactly proof, though," said Sasha. "I mean, it *was* garbage night after all. It's no big surprise for someone to take an extra bag out."

"Anyway, it doesn't matter," said Serena. "All that does is that we *are* sensing things, and we need to make notes, however small." Serena sat and tapped the pen against her chin. "So the visions could come true anywhere from hours to months afterward. Maybe if we research the experiences of other psychics we might find out more about how premonitions work." She reached for the laptop.

"Other psychics? Since when are we officially psychics?" Sasha scoffed, turning away and rearranging her makeup on the dressing table then picking up a lip balm and sliding it across her lips.

"Since we sensed things that came true!" Serena's voice went up an octave.

Talia placed her hand on the laptop screen and closed it just as Serena opened it. "Leave the research till later; let's hold hands again and see if anything happens." There was a slight twinkle in her eye.

"Oh great, more stinky smells to put up with. If I faint, I blame you, Talia." Sasha held out her hands, her silver fingernails glittering under the light like ten little stars. "And we need to come up with a better term to use instead of 'holding hands.' It sounds like we're kids getting ready to cross the road."

Except with this, we didn't know what we'd see on the other side.

"Good idea. Let's say that we're...*connecting*. How about that?" Talia raised her eyebrows in satisfaction. Another name for something, another term to give certainty to the uncertain—to enhance and grab hold of whatever small thread of control she could find.

Sasha shrugged and nodded. "That'll do."

We took hold of each other's hands and *connected*, waiting for the bubbly sensation. What came instead was a loud bang and my heart skipped a beat.

Serena screamed. "What on earth was that?"

We dashed to the window and yanked open the drapes. A bright ball of yellow hung in the sky farther down the road. It looked to be coming from the main street of town. Smoke billowed out and up into the night sky, and I jumped as another bang exploded and more yellow—orangey yellow—filled the sky. "Holy crap!"

My heartbeat tripled and Mom came rushing in. "Oh my God, what *was* that?"

"It's a fire, somewhere in town." Serena's voice shook. "I can't believe it." She looked at me and I shook my head and mouthed "no."

"What do you think it is? What's on fire?" Sasha peered through the window. "Can we go look?"

"No!" Mom said. "We'll stay here where it's safe."

Fire engine sirens rang in the distance, and Serena rubbed her ears.

"But, Mom, I won't be able to sleep not knowing where it was," said Sasha. "Can't we take a quick drive? We don't have to go that close."

"Yeah, I want to know, too," I said. There'd be no way I'd sleep after this. Serena was right. Somehow, we *were* psychic in our own unique, fragmented way.

Mom pursed her lips to one side, and I could tell that although she was trying to protect us, she was also curious. "Well, all right then. Just a quick drive. But only close enough to see where it is, that's all. I'm sure we'll find out the details on the news." She turned away from the window. "C'mon, let's go before I change my mind."

CHAPTER 5

Most of our neighbors were outside peering at the smoke and fire lighting up the night sky, although I couldn't see Riley or Mr. Jenkins. Mom drove cautiously around the streets leading to town, as though scared another fire might suddenly ignite nearby. Sasha was checking Twitter on her phone to see if anyone was tweeting about it. We pulled into a parking spot alongside the harbor and got out of the car.

"Is it a shop?" Mom asked no one in particular, her brows furrowed as she tilted her head sideways to see behind the row of buildings along the main street. "I think it's behind the post office."

"I can feel the heat from here," Talia said, then quickly glanced at me to see if I could feel it too and it wasn't just her heightened sense. I reassured her that I could.

We crossed the main road to a gathering of people on a corner, all staring at the blaze across and farther up the intersecting road. Now the heat was more noticeable. A fire fighter motioned for everyone to stay back. Smoke obscured much of the view, but the images I'd seen during the vision at school flashed through my mind.

"What's on fire?" Mom asked a stranger.

"The liquor store."

Alcohol. Tamara had tasted it, and I'd seen a bottle rolling along the ground.

"Oh, gosh. What a waste," said Mom.

"The building was old and run down anyway."

"I meant the wine." Mom smiled. "But as long as no one was hurt, that's the main thing."

"Doesn't appear to be. The store would have closed an hour ago; the town's practically deserted at this time of night." The stranger, a woman about fifty, eyed my mother. "New here, huh?"

Mom nodded.

"We don't normally welcome new residents with such a grand show." She smiled. "Anyway, I think they have it under control. Too-do-loo." The woman turned and walked in the other direction, her skirt flapping in the breeze wafting across from the harbor.

A few people filmed the scene on their phones; many hands covered mouths in shock, and others exchanged "oh dears" and "can you believe its" and "not agains."

Wait. *Not again?* Had something like this happened before?

Despite the fire being farther up the road, the radiant heat warmed my face; it was like standing near a heater. My hot eyes stung, but not as much as earlier that day. We'd seen this, predicted it in a way, and yet we'd been unable to prevent it. I glanced at Serena who wore a worried, almost guilty expression.

"Why would we foresee something like this if we weren't able to stop it? It's not fair," she whispered. "I feel partly responsible."

Talia tugged her backward a little, not wanting anyone to overhear.

"My thoughts exactly," I said, frustration gripping at my chest. "I don't understand what good these visions are if we can't do anything about them or don't get enough information to help us figure them out."

"Maybe we *are* just warming up, as Talia suggested," Serena proposed.

"Ha. Literally."

"Shh," Talia mouthed. "We'll discuss this later."

I glanced toward Mom, busily chatting with another stranger. *Maybe we should tell her, especially after tonight.* The pros and cons of doing so swung back and forth in my mind like a pendulum.

"I wish there was something we could do, I feel so helpless." Tamara hung her head.

"I wish there was something we could have *done*," Sasha whispered.

"Do you think it was deliberately lit?" I asked, glancing toward a police officer talking to a couple of people.

Sasha shrugged. "Probably. How would a fire just start suddenly if no one was there?"

Despite the heat, a shiver rolled up my spine. What if it was deliberate and the culprit was standing right here in this crowd of people? Didn't arsonists like to watch the results of their destruction? I swiveled side to side, suddenly vulnerable. What if it was that nice lady Mom had spoken to? *C'mon, don't be silly, Savannah!*

An elbow dug into my ribs. I turned to Serena, who tipped her head subtly to the right. Following her gaze, my eyes homed in on Riley Pearce, whose dark features matched the night. He strode through the crowd and paused when he got near me.

"We meet again," he said, then glanced at my sisters. "Do you go everywhere with your sisters?"

My insides clenched. "No, of course not. But what do you care, anyway?"

"Just curious. Every time I see you, there's a sibling entourage."

If he was trying to be funny, it wasn't working.

"I take it you're an only child?" I crossed my arms. Did he think I was some kind of baby because I spent time with my sisters? It was often just practical to go places together, that's all.

"What makes you say that?"

I shrugged.

"Not that it's any of your business, but I have a brother." He rubbed the back of his neck and turned to look at the fire. "So, out here watching the show, huh?" The fire's reflection licked at his face, highlighting his golden skin and making it appear waxlike.

"We wanted to see where the fire was and make sure no one was hurt." I looked toward the fire too, my gaze meeting Mom's along the way as she listened to whatever the stranger was saying. She caught sight of Riley next to me, and, probably assuming he was the so-called boy I liked—thanks to Sasha—raised her eyebrows, nodded, and gave me a thumbs-up. *Mom!* God, she was embarrassing. *I hope he didn't see!*

"No one's been hurt in any of the fires so far," Riley said matter-of-factly.

What had one of the onlookers said before? *Not again.*

"Do you mean there've been other fires in town?"

"Wow, you *are* a newbie, aren't you?" Riley shifted his weight onto one foot and relaxed the other in front of it. "New Year's Eve, a few cars. Could've just been a couple of drunken idiots, but a week later there was a fire at the doctor's office, followed by one in some guy's backyard shed. They found evidence of accelerants at the scenes. This is the biggest one yet." He gestured to the fire, which was dwindling somewhat with the thick streams of water bursting forth from the fire fighters' hoses. "And obviously, being a liquor store, the whole place was one big accelerant."

"You seem to know a lot about all this."

"I keep informed." He crossed his arms. "At least the fire's provided some excitement for the night."

I stepped back. "Excitement? Are you crazy? Someone could have been hurt. How is that exciting?" My skin burned more at his insensitivity.

"Look, the fire damage is done. We can't change what's happened. But you've got to admit, it's a pretty spectacular sight." He put his hands on his hips and surveyed the scene, flames still dancing, smoke still billowing upward.

"I don't agree." I eyed him with curiosity. "How is this spectacular? You like fire or something?"

His head turned from the direction of the fire to face me and our eyes connected. "Oh, you don't think I had anything to do with it, do you?" He laughed, and his Adam's apple bobbed up and down. "I've been working all night." He pointed down the main street. "Video store. Just came

60

out to see what the explosion was."

It was then that I noticed his Video Village uniform. "Ah. Right." Maybe I'd get my sisters to choose the DVDs if we wanted to rent any sometime. No doubt he'd find a way to poke fun at whatever movie I'd choose. "So, a video store. Not the best job security for the long term, is it?"

"Job security? You think I want to keep working at a video store all my life?" Creases of irritation lined his face.

"What I meant was you wouldn't be able to. They'll be extinct soon with so many people downloading movies instead."

"True, but there's also many people that *don't*. And *they* come to the store," he replied. "I'm only working there for some cash. Once school is done, I'm outta there and outta this town."

"On to bigger and better things, huh?"

"Something like that."

I was surprised none of my sisters joined in the discussion, especially Sasha, but they seemed more interested in watching me battle it out with him. "Well, what are you hanging around here talking to me for? You better get back to your job before they fire you." I stuck my thumb over my shoulder in the direction of the video store.

"Ha! *Fire* me." He glanced toward the blaze. "If you're trying to be funny, it's not working."

Didn't I just think the same thing about him? Weird.

"I hope you're prepared for Saturday, Volleyball Girl." He winked and walked off with an air of confidence and entitlement like he owned the town. He didn't seem the least bit shocked by the fire either. Saturday. The volleyball match. *Oh, what have I gotten myself into?*

As my mind filled with nervous regret, Mom gathered us all together and we crossed the road, heading back to the car. Mom told us about three new friends she'd made in the crowd, one of whom was a single mother like her. As I slid into the backseat of Mom's minivan, I glanced back along the street; the moon was pale in comparison to the remaining flames and hazy glow of the streetlamps. Another shiver crept up my spine. Standing in the park opposite the row of shops, hands in pockets, and gaze directed straight at the fire, was Mr. Jenkins.

CHAPTER 6

This was it. My last shot. My last chance to prove to Riley "Hotshot" Pearce I was no one-hit wonder. My eyes squinted at the sun's rays, but I kept focused on my target, shifted my weight back a little, and propelled the ball over the net. My thumb throbbed in time with my heartbeat. Riley leapt sideways and stretched his arm up high, his body was one lean length of skin, muscle, and power, but it was no match for my mean serve. Sand sprayed outward where the ball landed. After Riley's last-chance momentum, he joined it on the ground.

Cheers roared from the sidelines, mostly from my sisters, barring Sasha, who was in hiding at home after burning her ear with the hair straightener. She had to wear a thick bandage in a circular lump around her ear till it healed. If she'd burnt the other ear as well she would have looked like Princess Leia.

My team high-fived me, and I absorbed the satisfaction of the moment. *Ah, victory.* Riley brushed sand off his skin and walked around the net. Part of me felt like saying, "Ha-ha, told you so, ner-ner, ner-ner, ner!" But words weren't necessary.

I expected him to say it was just a fluke, and I'd have to join them for another match next weekend, but he simply held out his hand. "Well done, Volleyball Girl," he said.

I eyed his tanned hand with blue ribbons of veins bulging underneath, noticing it was just like the hand in my vision that turned the doorknob. I grasped it, and hot skin warmed mine as he gave me a firm, brief shake. "Looks like you live up to your nickname after all."

I smiled. "Thanks, but it's not a name I'm that aching to live up to."

"I could always call you 'Newbie' instead."

"Or, here's an idea," I planted my hands on my hips, "you could call me Savannah."

His lips attempted a grin, and he shaded his eyes from the sun as he turned away. "See you round, Volleyball Girl."

Little did he know just how much *I* was seeing.

• • •

"Are you sure I look okay?" Mom asked, twirling in front of the mirror in her bedroom, the scent of floral perfume filling the air. "Or should I change back into the black outfit? Black might be more suitable for a first date, what do you think?"

"Mom, black is not your color. I'd stick with the bluey-purple—it brings out your blue eyes," I reassured.

"Thanks, darling." She smoothed her hands down her gray pants and adjusted the sleeves of her bluey-purple shirt. "More perfume?"

"No," said Sasha, whose sense of smell had heightened recently, even when we weren't having visions. She could barely be near the kitchen whenever meat or fish was cooking.

"Mom, you look great, you smell great, and we'll be fine here on our own. Go and have a good time." Talia ushered her out of the room before she decided to change outfits, redo her hair, or, heaven forbid, do the dishes.

Knock, knock!

"Oh God, he's here! Um…" Mom spun this way and that, as though she'd forgotten which direction the door was in. "Right. Okay. Time to go. Um…"

"Mom!" Talia said. "Take a deep breath and answer the door."

She did as she was told and opened the door to reveal a brown-haired man in dark jeans and a nice blue shirt. He had that rugged appearance that men of the trades often had—rough-looking hands, sun-kissed skin, and a hint of stubble across his jaw. Sasha stepped back a bit as a heady scent of spices wafted inside. It'd been a while since a masculine scent had been welcomed into our home, and I held onto the wall for a moment in a wave of light-headedness, suddenly aware of the painful absence of my father again.

"Rose, you look lovely," Wayne said. "And these must be your beautiful daughters." He smiled and eyed us all one by one.

"Hi," I said. "I'm Savannah."

"And this is Sasha, Serena, Tamara, and Talia," Mom added, and I'm sure he would forget our names in the next minute or so. Sometimes people used to call us the triplets and the twins to be able to keep track of who we were. Tamara and Talia's hair was a much lighter brown than our dark brown hair, and Tamara, with the natural highlights of blond in her curls, had taken after Mom the most, whereas my triplet sisters and I were like Dad through and through.

"It's great to meet you all. And wasn't it lucky your Mom needed car help? Otherwise, we may not have met." He smiled at her with a genuine sense of admiration.

Wow, he really liked my mom. This was really happening. Mom's first date since…losing Dad. She looked more nervous than Serena, who was huddled behind Sasha.

"Shall we?" Wayne asked, crooking his elbow. Mom visibly swooned and hooked her arm in his.

"Bye, girls. Be good, and I'll see you later tonight." She waved with her free hand and Wayne opened the door to his car for her. I didn't know the make and model or anything, but it was a true guy's car and polished to within an inch of its life.

I closed the front door as they drove off, and then turned to my sisters. "So, house to ourselves, what should we do?" I rubbed my hands together, Tamara style.

"How about we get out the Ouija board?" Talia's eyes sparkled.

"No way," said Serena. "You've got to be kidding."

"Then why don't we *connect* and see if anything shows up?" said Talia. "We haven't seen much since the fire, except Sasha's ear-burning incident, and a weird argument between unknown people."

"I don't feel like doing it yet," replied Tamara. When it came down to it, none of us really wanted to see something bad that we wouldn't be able to prevent. "But what I do feel like is a nice hot slice of pizza. Who's with me?"

My stomach grumbled at the word. "Mmm, sounds nice."

"Then let's go get some."

"What, you're not going to cook it from scratch?" asked Sasha, her hair perfectly straight and sleek, the look spoiled by the bandage on her ear.

"Nah, let's get it down the road." Tamara grabbed the cash Mom had left for us on the coffee table. "Who wants to come with me?"

"Not me." Sasha flopped on the couch. "Not while I look like Princess Leia's mutant sister."

I laughed. *My thoughts exactly*, though I hadn't told her that. "I'll go." I grabbed my phone and shoved it in my pocket, pausing at the front door when a slamming sound came from across the road. I peered through the window. A guy with hair shaved so close to his head that it looked more like a shadow, marched out of the house. Riley's brother?

Riley opened the door and came after him. "Well, excuse me for being under eighteen!" he yelled.

"Just leave it, Riley. I need some space!" The guy approached his car and opened the door.

"Leave then, I don't care! I'll look after myself like I've always done." Riley crossed his arms and his brother got in the car, slammed the door, and sped off down the road. Riley watched him go then banged his fist against the porch railing.

Talia, standing next to me, flinched. "I felt that the other night. That pain on my fist."

"So this was *their* argument we sensed," I stated. I'd only seen the angry face of the brother, his soundless words launching from his mouth and his arms flailing about. His hand running over his head and grabbing the car keys before slamming the door behind him. Serena had said they were fighting about money and something to do with not being able to get a job out of town.

"Maybe that's why he's such a jerk sometimes," said Talia. "Trouble at home?"

"Who knows," I replied. I'd never seen anyone but him around the house and had only seen the assumed brother that day. Riley Pearce was a mystery to me.

We waited until he'd gone back inside then eased the door open. "Back soon," I said, and Tamara and I walked out to pick up our dinner from the pizza shop a few minutes away.

• • •

"Don't eat it yet, wait till we get home," I said, elbowing Tamara in the ribs as we carried the pizza boxes.

She put the slice back in the box. "Ah, that smell. Nothing like it."

There *was* something amazing about pizza smell. Hopefully it wouldn't cause Sasha to faint when we got home, although I was sure it would only have her salivating. We rounded the corner onto Roach Place and my stomach flipped a little. Riley sat on the edge of the curb outside his house, tossing pebbles into the stormwater drain.

Tamara cleared her throat, leaned close to me, and whispered, "Might be a good chance to see what's going on. See if there was a reason we sensed his argument in our vision." She cocked her head toward Riley and my lips tightened.

"Why me?"

"You're the one he seems to talk to the most."

I *was* curious. He annoyed the hell out of me, but he'd

been a good sport at the volleyball match that day. Maybe I should try and find out more about him; he was our neighbor after all. Not that I particularly wanted to find out more about Mr. Jenkins; that guy gave me the creeps.

"Nice evening," Tamara said, glancing up at the sky, its subtle pink glow preparing its transition to dusk.

Riley gave a simple nod and tossed another pebble.

"I'll just take these inside." Tamara grabbed the box from my hands and left me standing there near Riley.

"Is everything all right?" I asked him.

"Yeah, why wouldn't it be?"

"I kind of overheard the argument. It looked fairly heated."

"Brothers fight—it's normal. No big deal."

"Try having four sisters, it's a nightmare sometimes."

"I can imagine."

"So," I moved a bit closer, "I haven't ever seen your parents around."

"That's because they're not around." Riley tossed a pebble across the road and it rolled into the stormwater drain. "Mom died a few years ago. Dad died last year."

Crap. I regretted opening up this can of worms, but at least it explained why he was so uptight all the time. "Oh man, I'm sorry. So it's just—"

"Me and my brother, yep. I'm not eighteen for about another nine months, so he's stuck here with me until I can legally move out on my own." Riley's gaze stayed fixed on the ground.

I sat on the edge of the curb next to him. "My dad's gone too." I picked up a pebble and mimicked his toss from before, but mine landed on the grass of our front lawn. "Well, we don't know if he's *gone* gone, but he's gone. Disappeared. Nine years ago."

Riley turned his head to face mine, his eyes wide. "Really? And you have no idea—"

"Where he is? No. No one does. It's a cold case now." I shifted on the edge of the curb but couldn't get comfortable. "And he didn't walk out on us, if that's what you're thinking."

"I wasn't thinking that."

"Because he wouldn't have done that. Something bad happened, we just don't know what."

Riley shook his head from side to side. "That sucks, big time."

"Yep." I noticed how much smaller he looked sitting there on the side of the road, his head hung low. "But at least, I mean, I don't know how I'd deal with—"

"Both parents gone?" We were making a habit of completing each other's sentences. "We manage. And at least I have some sort of closure, I guess."

Unlike me.

Riley eyed me with an expression akin to a foreigner recognizing one of his own in unfamiliar territory. "Maybe we have more in common than I thought, Volleyball Girl."

"Maybe we do," I replied. "And it's Savannah." I smiled. Although it was better than what I used to be called. *That poor Delcarta girl with the aneurysm.* I remembered the looks of pity on the faces of those around me when I'd been diagnosed. "That poor girl, no guarantee she'll survive the operation, let alone the condition," I'd overheard someone say when I went into a store to pick up a block of chocolate two days before the operation. If I was going out with a bang, I wanted to indulge in my favorite food first.

My stomach grumbled, and I turned to Riley. "You eaten dinner?"

"Nah, haven't had a chance to think about it."

I tilted my head toward our house. "We have plenty of pizza...you wanna, like, come inside or something?"

"I couldn't, your sisters hate me."

"They'll survive. You've gotta eat." I nudged him in the arm. *Why did I do that? He probably thinks I'm an idiot!*

"Thanks, but I don't want to intrude."

I glanced at the light shining through our front window, and my stomach grumbled again. "Wait right here." I got up and adjusted my denim shorts, and then walked across the road to our house. I was certain Riley's eyes were glued to my behind. A couple of minutes later I emerged, carrying a cardboard box of pizza and a couple of napkins. "I hope you like supreme," I said as I approached Riley on the curb, and my eyes tingled as a never-before-seen expression graced his face: a genuine, grateful, and gorgeous smile. Supreme indeed.

CHAPTER 7

"Seriously, how can you girls create so much garbage?" Mom lifted the plastic bag and tied it in a knot at the top. "I just took some out, now there's more." She lugged it over to the front door. I noticed Riley's garbage cans weren't yet out.

"Um, here, Mom. I'll take it." I took the bag from her hands, and she returned to the kitchen to chop vegetables while Tamara sautéed onions in a pan. It was a later-than-usual dinner as Mom had been to a longer-than-usual play rehearsal.

"Well, aren't you going to take it out?" Sasha asked, her feet propped up on the coffee table and eyes glued to a reality show on the television.

"Oh, I just remembered I have some more stuff to throw out from my room." I scurried off and peered out my bedroom window. A light glowed in the front of Riley's house and a faint shadow moved across it. *I wonder what he's doing. What he's thinking? Hang on, what am I thinking? Why am I thinking about what he's thinking about? God, Savannah!*

The light on his front porch came to life and his door opened. A barefoot Riley, in a loose tank top and shorts, carried a garbage bag and swung it into the can. I dashed out of the bedroom and to the front door, slowing down upon walking outside. Pure coincidence we happened to be taking the garbage out at the same time, pure coincidence. Riley wheeled his garbage can to the curb as I walked over to ours, already standing there in waiting.

"Well, hello. What a coincidence," Riley said, and I held back a grin.

"We forgot to put this out." I lifted the heavy bag an inch, and Riley strolled across the road.

"You girls must have triple the garbage that we have; big families aren't that great for the environment, are they?"

"You sound like my mother."

"Ouch. That's not something a guy wants to hear —*ever*."

I smiled. "Too late." I lifted the lid and with two hands, heaved the bag in and flipped the lid closed.

"Two hands huh, that heavy? Or are you not as good at lifting weights as you are at volleyball?" He rested his hands on his hips in a totally manly I'm-so-confident way.

"Is that supposed to be a compliment or an insult?"

"What do you want it to be?"

"Why are you answering my question with a question?" I crossed my arms.

"Why are you answering *my* question with a question?"

Heat burned up the back of my neck and crept onto my face. "Maybe you would have used two hands as well. Us girls do have triple the garbage, remember?"

"Fair enough." He grinned. "But where are those

muscles responsible for your mean serves?" He came closer and prodded my bare arm then lifted it up into a bodybuilders pose. "C'mon, show me whatcha got."

I squeezed my bicep to make it bulge, and he pressed on it with warm hands. "There. That good enough for you?" I asked. He released my arm and I let it flop to my side, and it seemed as if I'd caught Talia's heightened sense of touch for a moment.

"Not bad." He nodded. "Let's see how they work." Riley leaned onto our closed garbage can with his elbow, his hand beckoning mine.

"What? You want me to arm wrestle with you? Outside, at night, on top of a garbage can?" This guy was crazy. Crazy, but addictive. I wanted nothing more than to grasp that hand and feel its warm buzz shooting up my arm and throughout my body. Damn, he was making me crazy too. I glanced around the empty street and toward my house where a faint smell of garlic and onions wafted through the screen door. "Fine. I'll wrestle you." I leaned on the lid. "Your arm, I mean." The heat on my face spread, and the corner of Riley's mouth twitched.

"Well, I wouldn't say no to other types of wrestling either." He chuckled.

Wow, was he hitting on me?

"That is, if I had to tackle you to save you from an oncoming car or something."

Ah, nice save, hotshot.

I wrapped my hand around his—almost twice the size of mine—and gripped it hard.

"I'll only use half my strength, make it easier for you."

"Aw, you're too kind," I said, and pushed down on his

hand, almost taking it to the lid until his biceps clenched and he yanked it back up.

"Hey! I didn't say start yet!" His gaze pierced through my eyes.

"I was just making sure you were paying attention, checking out your reflexes." And *my* reflexes, according to my neurologist following the operation and coma, were perfect, thank you very much.

"Sure you were. You were trying to catch me off guard and win by default."

"Whatever you say." I shrugged. "So, when are we starting then? Next week, next month? I don't have all—"

"Now!" He pushed against my hand, and I countered his pressure with my own. It felt like my hand was about to snap off.

"Hey!" I said through gritted teeth.

"I was just making sure you were paying attention, checking your reflexes, you know," he said.

I gripped and pushed harder, my arm at a forty-five-degree angle in the wrong direction. "You seem to like copying what I say." I grunted. "Can't you think of smart words all by yourself?" The corner of his mouth rose further and he didn't attempt a response. "Cat got your tongue?" It was hard to speak but I wanted to give it everything I had, show him I was no wuss, no girly-girl who couldn't take on a challenge. Of course his muscles and strength were probably five times that of mine, and maybe he was only using slight force, but my arm held strong. Sweat tickled my forehead and I hoped it wasn't visible. I darted my gaze briefly to just over his left shoulder. "Who's that?" I asked, forcing a look of concerned curiosity.

"Who's who?" He moved his head slightly to look and—bam! I pushed his hand over and down onto the garbage can lid.

"Gotcha!" I let go and stepped back. Riley glanced back at me with a scowl on his face.

"You playing tricks on me, Volleyball Girl?" He leaned both his elbows onto the lid, his hands forming a pyramid under his chin.

"Winning isn't only about strength; it's about tactics." I'd learned that the hard way. When all strength is gone, the only thing you have to keep you going is your mind.

"Is that so?" he asked. "Anyway, I was going to let you win."

I flashed a suspicious grin. "Oh yeah, sure."

"But I plan to beat you soon at volleyball. You wait and see. I've just been letting you have your moment first. Then I'll strike when you least expect it. Tactics, remember?"

"So, do I get a prize for winning the arm wrestle?" I raised my eyebrows.

Riley glanced around, as though a trophy might suddenly appear. He patted his pockets and pulled something out. "Here, how about a Tic Tac?"

"What flavor?"

"Peppermint."

I suddenly remembered Tamara's vision, or *taste*-ion. "Something minty, like a Tic Tac or Mentos."

I held out my hand and he tipped a couple of the tiny pellets onto my palm.

"Tic Tacs for your tactics." He grinned.

"Gee, you're a funny guy." Actually, he kinda was, in a crazy way. I popped them into my mouth and slid the minty flavor around my tongue. I tipped my chin, gesturing to his house. "So, where is your brother tonight?"

"Working. He's a chef."

"My sister wants to be one of those. I couldn't imagine anything worse, no offense. The idea of being stuck in a kitchen is not for me."

"Me neither. I need to move."

"Me too."

Strangely, we both stood there as still as the garbage cans. "Well," I flung my thumb behind me and twisted my upper body, "I think the family chef is probably just about done with dinner." A flash of something caught the corner of my eye. I twisted again, and the face of Mr. Jenkins disappeared behind the drapes in his window, gray smudges of clouds stretching across the darkening sky above his house. I turned back to Riley. "So, what's the deal with him?"

"Mr. Jenkins?"

Did Riley know he'd been looking at us through the window? If he did, he hadn't shown any indication of being bothered.

"He keeps to himself. The only time he says anything is in class, and even then it's only the necessary stuff."

"Gives me the creeps."

"Really? I never thought of him that way. I always just thought he was a bit of a loner. He's been worse since his wife died."

"Oh, he was married?"

"Yep. She died not long before my dad." Riley's head dropped a little. "Don't know all the details. It was all hush-hush, something about bleeding in the brain. Whether she fell or had a condition, I'm not sure."

A ripple of familiarity rolled through me. Bleeding in the brain, a possible consequence of having an aneurysm. I could still hear the doctor's words when he explained the risk of not going through with the operation. Funnily enough, the risk was the same with *going* through the operation. Don't have it and I could die, have it and I could die. Coin toss anyone?

"Oh, that's sad. Poor woman."

"Maybe Roach Place is where everyone who's lost someone ends up." Riley pointed to the house at the end of the cul-de-sac. "The couple who live there lost their little girl a few years ago."

Geez. I knew Roach Place had a bad ring to it. What was this? Death Row? "That's awful." I shivered.

"Yeah." Riley shoved his hands into his pockets. "Anyway, enough of this depressing talk." Riley's chest rose with a sharp breath. "Like you said, your dinner is probably ready, and I'm sure you need to rest after the effort of our arm wrestle."

"Ha-ha. I think you're the one who needs to rest after I slammed your hand onto the lid, remember?"

"Oh, it hurts so bad." His face scrunched up as though in agony.

One minute he was all serious, and the next, his snarky self was back. Just who was Riley Pearce underneath this facade?

CHAPTER 8

Tamara plucked a selection of vegetables and fruit from the produce store, and we paid for them and walked out onto the main street, which was busy with Saturday shoppers and tourists and people needing their afternoon coffee fix. We passed the newsstand where newspapers displayed out the front had the headline "Who is Burning Our Town?" and a picture of the flaming liquor store. Tamara and I exchanged glances, and I knew she was thinking the same thing. Why? Who? And will we see another one and be unable to stop it?

I peered discreetly into Video Village as we passed it. After the day's volleyball match, Riley had mentioned he'd be starting work late in the afternoon, but he wasn't there.

"Checking out the new releases or hoping to check out something else?" Tamara asked.

Oops, I thought I was being discreet. "No, not looking at anything."

Tamara laughed. "It's okay, you know; you're allowed to like him. He's hot."

"Just because he's hot is no reason to like him."

"But it's an understandable reason."

"Maybe *you* have the hots for him, huh?"

"No way. But, have you seen his brother? I caught him coming home late one night when I was up getting a drink of water. Phwoar!"

"He's a chef, you know."

"No way, really?" Tamara's face lit up like a Christmas tree. "Ooh, that makes him way hotter. Do you know where he works? We should totally go there to eat."

"No, why don't you ask Riley?" I asked. My eyes fixed ahead on the dark-haired guy in a Video Village shirt walking our way.

Tamara gasped. "Don't say a word," she whispered.

"Hi, Tamara. Volleyball Girl," he said, nodding at each of us.

"Are you ever going to call me by my real name?" I narrowed my eyes.

"Maybe, maybe not."

"Maybe if you win the next volleyball game you can start calling me Savannah then."

"Maybe I'll just keep letting you win, then."

"Whatever you say."

"So, any exciting plans for tonight? What are the Delcarta girls up to?" he asked.

For a split second I thought he'd called us the Delta Girls and almost choked on my tongue. What would he think if he knew what we could do?

Tamara answered, "Our Mom's new boyfriend is coming over for dinner. Should be—"

"Interesting," I said.

"Yeah, interesting. Not so sure about exciting. Well, maybe for Mom."

"Good for her," he said. "Can I interest you in a new release movie for afterward?"

"Oh, Savvy was just checking them out through the window, weren't you?"

"Sort of. Nothing much I want to see though." *Bloody hell, Tamara. Keep it up and I'll tell Riley you like his brother.*

"There're some good ones coming out next week. What do you like? Comedy? Thrillers?"

"Um, a bit of both."

"There's that one about the psychic cop, supposed to be good. I like the ones I can escape reality with. What about you?"

Ha. Escape reality? *Whose* reality? If only he knew.

"Ooh, that sounds like one all of us would like, Savvy. We'll have to get it," said Tamara.

I would have nudged her in the ribs, but it would have been too obvious. "So, Riley, where does your brother work?"

"My brother? Why?"

I could practically feel the heat radiating from Tamara's face.

"Um, just if we need a good place to eat."

"Oh, right. He works at Harborside, up on the hill." He pointed behind. "If you go, tell him I sent you. Maybe he'll give you a discount." Riley winked.

"Cool, thanks," I replied.

"Well, truckloads of entertainment-hungry customers must be waiting for me. Enjoy tonight. Hope the dinner does turn out to be exciting after all." He walked off and into the video store. I didn't know about dinner being exciting, but what we planned to do afterward could sure as hell turn out to be.

• • •

My stomach grumbled as the mouth-watering aroma of crusty bread fresh from the oven wafted up my nose. I placed the breadbasket on the table, resisting the urge to tear off a piece and devour it in one swallow. A flame licked at the wick of a candle as Sasha held the lighter toward it. It bobbed and glowed, catching the whooshes of air as we bustled around the table in preparation for the night's guest. I adjusted the napkins and made sure everything looked perfect, and my gaze drew to the flame again. Amazing how something so small and beautiful could become so big, so engulfing, and so destructive. One flame—that's all it took.

Knock, knock!

"I'll get it," I said, as Mom popped her head out of the kitchen with eyes wide and eager. I turned the handle and stepped back as the door swung inward. Wayne's mouth turned up into a smile.

"Hi there…"

"Savannah," I said, as his voice strung out, obviously trying to remember which Delcarta daughter I was.

"Savannah, of course. It was on the tip of my tongue." He winked. "I'd shake your hand, but…" He lifted a bunch of rich, purple irises in one hand, and a box of chocolates in the other.

I smiled. "No problem, come on in." I stretched my arm out in a welcoming gesture and stepped aside as he entered.

"Hello…"

"Sasha," my sister said.

"Sasha, yes." He smiled and nodded, and then greeted Serena and Talia as they stepped forward and reminded him of their names too.

Tamara walked out from behind the kitchen, patting her hands on the white apron around her waist.

"And through the process of elimination, I guess you're Tamara," he said with a slight chuckle in his voice.

"That's me," she replied. "I'm always the one eating, cooking, or with some kind of food remnant unknowingly on my face," she added, wiping her cheek.

"So you're the chef for tonight, I see?"

"Well, along with Mom. She did most of the work."

Mom appeared from behind the kitchen too, her rosy cheeks matching her red dress and doing her name justice.

"Rose." Wayne approached her, his gifts outstretched. "You look lovely."

Her glow intensified, and she took the flowers and chocolates off his hands. Then he leaned in and pecked her on the cheek. Serena turned her head away from the public display of affection. Okay, so it was weird, but kinda cute. It amused me to see Mom behaving like a love-struck teenager. *Like me*, a voice inside said, but I pushed the thought away.

"Wayne, they're lovely, and appropriate," Mom said. Apparently, Iris Harbor was named after an early settler, a gardener and florist, who grew the most beautiful irises. Irises that continued to grow and bloom in the historic grounds of his house overlooking the harbor. Of course he was no longer alive, his house and garden maintained by others and a place where tourists flocked. Some say the name also originated from the iris-colored glow that appears on the ocean at dusk, yet no one knew why the ocean had a different appearance than elsewhere.

"I'll get those in some water," said Talia, retreating to the kitchen and returning moments later with a vase, placing it on the table next to the bread.

"Here, Wayne, have a seat." Mom pulled out a chair for him.

"Thank you. Shouldn't I be the one pulling out chairs for you?" he asked.

Mom blushed again. "Oh, nonsense. You're our guest. I'll just help Tamara bring out the meal." Mom scurried off and returned with a casserole dish, steam billowing up and clouding her face. Tamara carried the second dish, and they placed them on the table. There was barely enough room for everything now the flowers had taken center stage.

"Smells delicious," Wayne said. "Does this meal have an official name?"

"It's *coq au vin*," Mom replied. "I hope you like chicken."

"I love it."

Tamara snapped a photo of the meal with her phone.

Wayne laughed. "Well, it *is* worthy of a photo, that's for sure." He smiled.

"It's for my Pinterest board. I like to keep records of what we've cooked," Tamara said. "Oh, and check out other people's recipes of course."

Wayne's brow furrowed slightly, and Mom said, "Pinterest. It's a picture sharing website apparently."

"Oh. Never heard of it until now. Sounds interesting."

Tamara smiled, and I reckoned she resisted the urge to say it was "pinteresting."

"Here, let me." Mom scooped up a couple of chicken

drumsticks along with the thick sauce and vegetables and ladled it onto Wayne's plate. "And can I pour you a glass of wine?" She pointed toward the kitchen. "Red, white, or beer perhaps?"

"Ah, no thanks. I'm not really a drinker," he said, placing his napkin on his lap. "To get a six-pack you need to avoid six-packs." He offered a crooked smile and patted his stomach, which, if it was anything like the subtle, yet sculpted muscles of his arms outlined by his shirt, would probably be firm and lean.

"Do you play any sports?" I asked, as Mom disappeared to the kitchen.

"Not exactly," he replied. "I prefer individual types of activity. Running and weight training, mostly. A bit of indoor rock-climbing."

"I like rock-climbing too. Is there a venue nearby?"

"Yes, a couple of towns away in Fern Ridge."

"I'll have to check it out sometime." If he was going to be Mom's boyfriend, at least we had something in common.

"Don't you think you've got enough sports going on with your volleyball and now soccer at school, Savvy?" Talia asked, and I shot her a narrowed glare. "You don't want to overdo things."

"Ah, she's young and healthy, why not make the most of it," Wayne said.

Thank you. Someone on *my* side for a change. Though, Mom hadn't told him I was recovering from something major.

"Here we go. I have apple cider or lemonade." Mom appeared holding a bottle in each hand. "Or there's juice in the fridge."

"Apple cider will be fine. Thanks, Rose."

Mom filled her guest's glass, then hers, then passed the bottles around the table. "So, girls, Wayne is going to be helping out backstage for the play, isn't that nice of him?"

"Oh, just helping out with bits and pieces, lifting props to the stage, making sure everyone knows when they're up, that sort of thing."

"I'm so looking forward to the night of the performance." Mom beamed.

"Me too," Wayne replied. "It's going to be a night to remember, what with this talented actress in our midst." He opened his palm toward Mom.

Sasha cleared her throat, and I wondered if he was sucking up or if he was this complimentary all the time.

"That's an interesting place for a bookcase," Wayne remarked, peering toward the fireplace-no-more in the living room.

I turned my head, and Serena piped up. "Most of those books are mine. I ran out of room on my own bookcase."

"Quite the reader, huh?" Wayne asked, and Serena nodded.

"I guess the previous owners didn't see much of a need for a fireplace," Mom said. "We've only lived here a short time, but I take it that it doesn't get too cold during winter."

"Not often, but it can."

"How long have you lived in Iris Harbor, Wayne?" asked Serena. This was a good sign. Maybe she was starting to accept that Mom was moving on. Or maybe she was just sussing out the guy.

Wayne tapped his chin. "Oh, a little over six months, since I scored the job at the garage. But I've passed through the town now and then. And I'm glad I passed through last year and found the permanent mechanic's position available." He glanced at Mom, the corner of his mouth curling upward.

Mom brushed a clump of curls off her face. "Well, dig in, everyone!"

• • •

When plates were emptied and Tamara and Talia took the casserole dishes to soak in the sink, Mom made coffee and invited Wayne outside on the patio. They sat on the two-seater wicker settee to watch the evening sky, and…er…have some alone time, I guessed. Which meant it was a perfect opportunity for us Delta Girls to connect.

"You coming, Serena?" I asked. My other sisters had already headed toward my bedroom.

She peered out the glass sliding door to the patio. "What do you think they're talking about?"

"Who cares, it's their business. C'mon."

"What if she marries him?"

"Serena! She's known the guy—what—less than a month?"

"But what if he's really keen and Mom's so lonely she jumps at the chance? You never know."

"I seriously doubt she'd jump into another marriage right away. Anyway, guys are usually scared of commitment," I said.

"Dad wasn't."

An awkward silence sat between us; every mention of his name was like a pinprick to the heart. I tugged her hand. "Well, remember *our* commitment to each other? It's time to connect while we've got the chance."

We joined our sisters, and Talia had already retrieved the vision journal from Serena's bedside drawer.

"Hey! Who said you could pry in my drawer?"

"I didn't pry, I just grabbed our journal." Talia tossed it onto her bed. "Anyway, what else could you have in there that you don't want us to see?"

"Nothing, but that's not the point." The drawer was slightly open, and she pushed it closed with her foot.

"Enough chitchat, let's do this." Tamara held out her hands. I grasped one and took hold of Talia's with my other hand, and we all joined together in a perfect circle.

I drew a deep breath and closed my eyes, my heart rate climbing with anticipation. We *could* see nothing, we could see boring garbage again, or we could see...

Oh.

What is that?

As a spark signaled an impending vision and bubbles fizzed up inside me, I saw...something. It was dark. Something moved slowly, right in front of my face. Blurry. A warm color and...lips. I could see lips and eyes and...oh my God.

Talia yanked her hand away from mine and my eyes shot open. "Whoa!" she exclaimed. "That was um...awkward. And...nice." Her cheeks flushed pink.

"Huh? All I heard was someone eating or slurping or... kissing?" Serena looked at Tamara, who with her sense of touch would have felt whatever we'd sensed.

"Um, yep. That would be it." Tamara cleared her throat and lowered her gaze to the ground.

"Oh, gross. I *thought* it was a male kind of smell,"

Sasha said, her face scrunched up. "Unless it was my future husband—ah...then it would be okay." She swooned, her hand on her heart.

"Oh God, do you think it was..." Talia's hand flew to her head. "Mom and *Wayne*?"

"Talia!" Sasha cried. "Puke!"

"Double puke." Tamara stuck her finger in her mouth and feigned throwing up.

"I knew it!" Serena said. "It's all happening. Mom's falling in love and Wayne's going to propose, and then he'll move in and we'll have no say in the matter and—"

"Serena, don't get ahead of yourself!" I grabbed her shoulders before she had a panic attack. "This...*kiss* might not happen for ages, and it might not be Mom at all."

"Well, she's the one sitting outside under the stars. Who else could it be?"

"Hang on—you've got the gift of sight, Savvy. Who did you see?" Sasha crossed her arms over her lacy top.

"Um." I shoved my hands in my pockets and shrugged. "Oh, I couldn't really see. It was dark, and, well...don't people close their eyes when they kiss?" I gulped, knowing too well who the kisser was. At least, I knew who *one* of the kissers was. As for the other participant, it could have been anyone, although I had a hunch. The lips, the eyes, the face I had seen in my vision belonged to Riley Pearce.

CHAPTER 9

One week later and there was not a kiss in sight. Not even any more visions. Maybe our abilities had fizzled out and run their course, or maybe there was nothing interesting in the future worth predicting. I might not have been able to control any of this stuff, but one thing I could control was myself. No freak illness or disease was going to get a grip on me ever again, uh-uh. If my mind could do what it had done when I'd connected with my sisters, who knew what else it could do? Who's to say my sheer determination and mind power couldn't be enough to keep me healthy and prevent any other problems?

As I walked onto the soft sand and traced the shoreline with my steps, I mentally grabbed the remaining fear that my aneurysm could return and bundled it into a tangled clump inside me. Then I ran. Not a slow, leisurely jog or a bouncy, aerobics kind of jog, but a full-on, hard-core, you-can't-catch-me run. Stuff the whole taking-things-slowly recovery mantra; my legs needed to move, and fast.

The sand crumbled and spread underneath my feet as I ran along the beach with my arms bent at right angles and hands like spears, cutting through the air. A rush of euphoria awakened my body, fueling it forward, as the landscape blurred around me. With each rapid exhalation, each whooshing of air from my lungs, I blew out a fragment of that clump of fear. *Breathe in—tear off a fragment, breathe out—expel the sucker. Repeat.*

The shrunken clump dissolved and disappeared into the atmosphere with a final whoosh. I slowed to a stop and doubled over, panting, and half laughing at the demise of my ball of fear. *Cheerio, you bastard. Good-bye, Adios, Sayonara.* Sweat drenched my top and dampened my hair, sticking it to the sides of my face as I fought to regain my breath. With my hands on my knees, I glanced up as the landscape swam into focus, as did something else. *Someone* else. Riley twisted and stretched along with a group of about eight others, before they broke away and sipped from water bottles, wiping their foreheads with towels. A few waved to each other and walked off, while Riley stood still, gulping his water then tipping it over his head; thin streams of water slithering down his muscled chest and abs.

Mmm…hello.

I straightened up and rested my hands on my hips as my breathing normalized. Well, as much as it could with *that* sight in front of me. Before I could pretend I was simply admiring the ocean view, his eyes caught mine. He raised his water bottle in a "Hi there" gesture, and then picked up his backpack and towel.

Okay, shows over. He's going home.

Oh, no he's not. He's…coming over here? Why did I have to be a sweaty mess at this moment? Oh well…looks like he is too. But it's so much more attractive on guys than girls.

"Hey there, Volleyball Girl." He dumped his bag and towel like he was about to set up camp. "You look hot."

"What?" I gulped.

He grinned. "Your face is red and you're all sweaty. We both must be crazy, exercising outdoors in this heat."

"Oh. Yes. We're not the only crazy ones." I cocked my head toward the group of people wandering off up the sandbank.

"Yeah, weekend boot camp. I join them whenever I'm not doing a shift at work." Riley's breathing was completely normal like he'd just woken from a nap, and I hoped he couldn't tell I was totally wiped out. I really should have built up to that kind of sprint, but the urge came out of nowhere, and, geez, I felt good inside. Clear. Light. Free.

Riley glanced toward the ocean; the afternoon sun was low and glaring on the horizon, bathing the water in a warm glow. "I'm going in." He tossed his water bottle onto his towel, walked to the water, and waded in to his waist. Then he turned around. "Well, you comin' or what?"

"Um…"

"You look like you could use it, Sweaty Girl."

"Gee, thanks. Is that my new nickname?" I crossed my arms.

"I might alternate between the two, depending on the situation." He smirked. "Well, don't just stand there."

"I didn't bring my swimsuit."

"It's only water; your clothes will dry." He gestured to my black tank top and denim shorts. "Unless you want to—"

"Don't even think about it!" I walked over, my clothes

staying right where they were supposed to be, and let the water cool my body as I stepped into the pulsing ocean. I dove underneath, washing away all the sweat and reminding myself that the fear was no longer allowed in. I'd changed the lock, and it didn't have the key. Yeah. Take that.

Treading water as subtle waves nudged around us, Riley's eyes narrowed. "So, why did you guys move here?"

"We just needed a fresh start, I guess." The truth was, the longer we stayed, the more Dad's absence cut into our hearts. That thought of, "What if he comes back today?" started each day as hopeful and ended it hopeless as another sunset returned us to darkness. "Iris Harbor seemed the perfect choice, Mom thought. Only an hour's drive back to our old house, and the benefit of being near the beach. And we didn't need to be close to the hospital anymore."

Crap. Didn't mean to say that.

"Hospital? Did your Mom work there or something?" Riley squinted as a warm beam of fading sunlight shone in his eyes.

"Um...not exactly. But she was there every day for a couple of months."

"She was sick? I didn't know."

"No, no she wasn't, it was..." I looked away, and as the water seemed strangely confining, I swam back to shore and stepped onto the wet sand. I may have killed the fear, but I hadn't killed the memories.

"Hey, you okay?" Riley followed, water dripping from his hair onto his face as he stepped out from the water.

"Yeah, yeah."

"Here." He handed me his towel, and I rubbed it over my body and ruffled the back of my hair with it.

I looked him in the eye. "She wasn't sick. I was."

Riley's eyes widened. "You? What was...Are you okay?"

A muscle in my arm tightened as he touched it. "Yeah, I'm fine now." I dried my legs and handed him the towel. He didn't bother drying himself, simply laid the towel on the sand and beckoned me to sit.

"Was it an injury or an illness?" he asked. "Sorry. You don't have to tell me. I'm just nosy like that."

I gazed at the ocean; gentle waves rolled in and out, back and forth, and the sky became a burnt orange as though it was remembering the liquor store fire. "I had an operation for an aneurysm. It's a sort of bulge in a blood vessel in the brain, so they had to fix it; otherwise, it could have..." I swallowed hard. "It could have ruptured. But there was a complication, and I didn't wake up from the anesthesia right away."

Riley's face froze in an expression of shock. "Oh, man. So how long were you out for?"

"Two months."

"Whoa. Like a coma?"

"Yep."

Riley ran his hand through his saturated hair. "That's... wow. And one day you just—"

"Woke up, yes." I nodded.

"How long ago was this?"

"I woke up three months ago."

Riley's mouth gaped open. "But...look at you. You're swimming and playing volleyball and—"

"Yeah, I know. So much for taking it easy." I smiled. "My family's been treating me like an invalid ever since. If they knew I'd gone for a run on the beach, they'd have me resting in bed all of tomorrow, just in case. But I feel fine."

"You're amazing." Riley's gaze connected with mine, and a buzz shot up my spine. I'd been called crazy, fragile, even *special* by my well-meaning family and friends whenever I tried to fit back into the life I had before, but never amazing.

Riley leaned closer, lifted his hand toward my face, and the vision I'd had flashed in my mind. *Oh my God, was this it? Was he going to kiss me?* His thumb, damp from the brief swim we'd had, swept across my cheek, and I resisted the urge to close my eyes. I wanted to see his face coming toward me, experience the thrill of anticipation, knowing exactly what was going to happen—but this time—in full sensory, high-definition 3D. No plastic glasses required.

Riley brushed my cheek with his thumb again, and then his lips parted. "You've got sand on your face," he said, brushing it off then returning his hand to his side of the towel.

Sand. That was it? No kiss? Or maybe it wasn't going to be me after all. "Oh, thanks." I gave it a brush of my own for good measure.

Riley picked up a shell and tossed it into the water with a smooth flick of his arm. "You've been through a lot."

"Yeah, I guess I have."

He tossed another shell. "Do you remember much of your dad? I mean, it was a long time ago, you said, but you would have been old enough to—"

"To know something bad had happened? Yes." To feel the pain and to go to bed at night and not understand why he couldn't be there to read me a story. "I remember snippets of things; he was always making us stuff: wooden toys or weird sculptures out of old bits and pieces. He'd pretend they had magical powers, and he'd make up stories about them. He was good with his hands, creating things, fixing things." My vision blurred a little. Was it from the sun's glare or the memories? "He owned a computer repair shop and worked hard, until one day he didn't come home. The police couldn't find any clues in his files but knew something must have happened suddenly because they found his computer still on, and he'd been halfway through typing an e-mail to his parents. He was telling them about a surprise trip he was going to take my mother on for their anniversary the following month. They never got the e-mail because he never finished it. The cops took a screenshot of it and gave it to my mother."

"I'm so sorry."

I shrugged. "We just have to move on, I guess. Easier said than done, though." Wow, I hadn't poured my heart out to anyone in like…forever.

Riley stood with another shell in his hand. He threw it hard, and it disappeared into the water. "It's not fair."

"I know, but we can't change what's happened."

Riley's body tensed. "It just sucks, all of it." He picked up a piece of driftwood and tossed it up and down in his hand. "It's not fair what happened to you, your dad, and…" he swung his arm back and over his shoulder, catapulting the driftwood far into the sea with the help of a grunt, "My selfish bastard of a dad!"

His outburst sent an uncomfortable jolt through me, and, by the looks of it, a flock of seagulls too; their white wings spread wide as they squawked and flew across the horizon. "What do you mean?" *Why would he speak that way about his dead father?*

He went to pick up another piece of driftwood but kicked it instead, sand spraying outward. "He chose not to live while my mother would have given anything *to* live. He disrespected her memory by doing the one thing that Mom fought so hard to resist."

Die? On purpose? Did he mean that his father...

Riley took his gaze off the ocean and focused it on me. The sadness in his eyes replaced the anger. He sat on the towel and rested his elbows on his knees. "In case you're wondering, yes, he committed suicide."

Holy crap. What was worse? Not knowing what happened to your father or knowing he took his own life? I had no words, but my hand found its way to his forearm, and he flinched then softened.

I must have looked like I wanted to hear more, or maybe he needed to let it all out and share the details he'd locked away for ages too, because he kept talking. "He suffered with depression after Mom died. We thought it would gradually get better as he dealt with his grief, but it only got worse." Riley shook his head and lowered it. "The counseling and medication didn't seem to do much; he became this bitter person I didn't recognize and said that life wasn't worth living without her in it. He didn't seem to realize that *we* were still here, and we needed him. We were hurting too, my brother and me, but he started getting angry with us all the time. We couldn't do anything right." He lifted his head and glanced at me. "Sorry. We were talking about you until I went off on a tangent about my own tragic life."

"Don't apologize, keep talking. Tell me what happened." I fixed my gaze on his tanned face. It was a little red from being in the sun all day, and there was a slight haze of darkness under his eyes.

"He didn't even think how Mom's death had affected us. Didn't even think how *his* death would affect us. My brother and I were going to seek some sort of intervention to force him into full-time psychiatric care, because we sure as hell couldn't do the job; but not long after, and without any sort of good-bye, he decided to drive himself off a cliff."

Oh my God. My hand covered my mouth.

"There were no other cars involved, no skid marks; he'd driven clean off the road and over the edge." He shot his hand forward to mimic the fatal crash, and I shuddered slightly as an image flashed through my mind of a car tumbling over the rocks. I blinked it away.

"I can't begin to imagine how hard this has been, Riley."

"Well, as you said, we can't change the past, can we? Have to keep moving forward." He fiddled with the fraying edge of his towel. "We both do."

I covered his fidgety hand with mine, hoping it wasn't too touchy-feely; but something told me he hadn't had any comfort in a long time and badly needed it. How much comfort my small hand could provide, I didn't know; but my heart was open wide for him right now. It was as though I could sense his pain. Or maybe my pain was merging with his—two souls on the same journey of grief.

His hand stilled, and I thought he might push it away; but instead he turned his palm upward and threaded his fingers between mine. I didn't want to cause any more pain, but I was curious about his mother. "Your mom, was she sick?"

He nodded. "Cancer."

"I'm sorry."

"She stayed positive; she was an inspiration. But

eventually it took hold, and she couldn't keep fighting. Before she died she told me not to waste a second of my life; she told me to make the most of the health that I had."

"Sounds like she was an amazing woman."

A faint smile touched Riley's face as he nodded. He twisted to the side and zipped open his backpack, withdrawing a black leather wallet. "Here, this is her."

He tilted the wallet toward me. A photo of his mother peeked out of the top of one of the credit card slots. Dark hair like his framed her face, falling about her shoulders in subtle waves. Her eyes were sharp, defined, but held softness in them too. She was grasping the pendant hanging from her necklace, something my own mother did when she had something on her mind; a more subtle version of the whole dishwashing obsession.

"She's beautiful," I said with a smile. "What was her name?"

Riley chuckled and put the wallet back in his backpack, and then turned to face me. "Her name was Savannah."

• • •

That night as I sat on the couch wedged between Mom and Serena, my feet propped up on the coffee table, a movie played out on the television screen. It wasn't nearly as interesting as my own life. I could barely focus; my mind was on other things after the intense afternoon I'd had on the beach. We'd connected, Riley and I. Not connected-connected like with my sisters, of course, but connected in a way that had taken us to a place where not a lot of damaged people got to go. A place where someone understood what you were going through, and understood the emotional rollercoaster ride your heart had a front row seat on with no safety belt: the anger, the frustration, the sadness, and the hopelessness. And somehow, our connection had an even greater impact on him.

I have the same name as his mother.

What were the chances? It wasn't like it was a really popular name. No wonder he couldn't call me anything but Volleyball Girl.

Riley had told me his mother was named after the place she was born. I told him I was named after no one—my mom and dad had just liked the name. So much for being significant! Mom had given us triplets names starting with *S* as a kind of novelty; she'd wanted to repeat what she'd done for my twin sisters, theirs starting with *T*. My breath halted in my throat for a second as I realized something: the first letter of our names corresponded to our psychic sense! Me with sight, Serena with sound, Sasha with scent, Tamara with taste, and Talia with touch.

Freaky.

This was starting to feel like more than coincidence. Maybe there *was* such a thing as fate, and, without knowing it, Mom had sealed part of that fate through the choice of our names. Or maybe I'd spent too long in the sun and was thinking up crazy crap. But maybe not. Tamara, the taste expert, loved food and cooking; and Sasha, my perfumeaholic sister had the gift of scent. Serena, well, she had taken up the violin last summer so that could be relevant, but what about Talia? I guess she was kinda good with her hands like Dad had been. Creative and crafty, practical, hands-on, so to speak. As for me, there wasn't anything specific, although I guess I was a visual learner. I needed to see things, experience things, in order to learn properly. Listening to a teacher—especially Mr. Weirdo Jenkins—rave on about molecules and whatever the layers of the earth were called, was not exactly my ideal way to discover the world around me. Put something interesting in front of my eyes and then I'd be all ears. Or eyes. Whatever.

A buzz disturbed my thoughts, and my gaze slid to my phone on the coffee table. It was on silent but the vibration against the wood had made its own sound. I picked it up and glanced at the text message. Riley. Only a few hours since I'd given him my number, and he was already texting me?

Hey VG, after u left I found ur earring on the beach. Can give it to u tomorrow, or do u want it now? Just got back from my friend's house so I'm right outside. R

I reached a hand to my left ear, the earring was still there, and then my right ear where I met only skin.

"You should turn off your phone, sweetheart. Relax and watch the movie," Mom said.

"Hang on, I'll just reply. It's only a Facebook notification." White lies never hurt anyone.

I tapped on the screen: *Hey, might as well get it now. Just come to my window, first one to the right of the front door.*

No point interrupting the family movie night with a visitor at the door, right?

I fake yawned. "I'm tired. I might head to bed now," I said.

"Oh, it's getting good. Don't you want to see what happens?" Serena asked, huddled in the corner of the couch with a cushion against her chest.

Hmm, I get enough of that without the help of Hollywood.

"Nah, you can fill me in tomorrow. Good night."

Mom kissed my cheek, and I traipsed to my bedroom and switched on the bedside lamp; its soft, warm glow cast an arched shadow behind the bed. I pulled back the drapes and saw Riley's silhouette a couple of feet away. He came closer as I wound the window lever around in circles, pushing the bottom part of the window outward. The house was so old it didn't have sliding windows, or even screens.

Riley ducked his head under the window and angled his body between it and the window frame until his face was just a ruler's distance from mine.

"Well, hand it over," I said with a grin.

He held up the earring then pulled it back. "Wait, do I get a reward for finding and returning your lost item?"

"I wouldn't count on it. Now gimme." I reached my hand out, but he pulled the dangling metal farther away.

"Wait. You have to prove yourself worthy. What is the name of the gemstone in your earring?"

I eyed the glossy black stone encased in a silver teardrop shape and hanging from a hook. "Um...a black one?"

He laughed, and I mouthed "shush" with a finger to my lips.

"No," he whispered, dangling the earring too far away for me to grasp it.

"Um...it's on the tip of my tongue. It's one of those, um, you know, the...black sort of...black things."

He shook his head. "It's an onyx."

I clicked my fingers together. "That's it!"

"Onyx is supposed to get rid of negative emotions and protect you," he remarked.

"Protect me from what?"

"You know, negative energies and stuff."

Was that really true? I'd only worn the earrings because they matched my black top. "Gee, you're a smart guy. Do they teach that sort of mumbo jumbo in geography or science class? Where did you learn about it?"

"Google." He grinned, and so did I.

"You Googled my earring?" I leaned on the window frame, giggling at his Googling.

He shrugged. "You learn something new every day."

"Who needs school when we have Google, huh?"

"Exactly. I also learned that onyx is supposed to improve self-confidence and enhance your senses."

I gulped. We didn't need any more sensory enhancement in this house, thank you very much. Hmm, maybe those earrings were somehow contributing to our psychic ability. Mom had given them to me when I got home from the hospital as a welcome home present. Nah, that wouldn't explain the vision we'd all had in the hospital. Maybe there wasn't *any* explanation at all; our gift could have randomly appeared for no reason whatsoever.

Riley curled his finger at me, drawing my head out the window. He lifted the earring to my ear and gently slipped the hook in place. His hand didn't move. It hovered near my ear, and then brushed against the sensitive skin beneath my earlobe. His gentle fingers traveled down my jawline, igniting a trail of tingles, until they stopped under my chin, holding it raised. His other hand approached and brushed the hair from my forehead, and his eyes bore deep into mine. That usual cocky cheekiness in his expression was nowhere to be seen; it was replaced by a serious, genuine, and raw hunger in his eyes. He cupped my cheeks in his hands and—*oh, here it comes!*—pulled my lips to his. Soft, warm, firm. I gripped the window ledge as a new sensation gripped me. Fresh, exciting, addictive. My first kiss—and it was just like heaven.

I didn't know how long it lasted; time seemed to stand still from the moment we touched. But when our lips parted ways, I wanted nothing but to be united with them again.

Riley smiled. His eyes were dark and glossy in the moonlight, his breath warm on my face. "So, does this mean you'll let me win at volleyball for a change?"

I smiled. "Not a chance."

"Then I'll just have to amp things up a bit, won't I?"

Was he talking about volleyball or us? Maybe both? "Two can play at that game."

"Two is my favorite number."

Mine too, now.

He stepped out from under the protruding window and lifted his hand in a wave. "I'll see you tomorrow." He slid his hands in his pockets and turned toward his house.

"Good night," I said.

He turned back. "Good night, Savannah."

CHAPTER 10

I didn't think I could get any happier. I didn't want to sleep, couldn't sleep, and I sure as hell didn't want to sit through another two hours of school lessons, especially as my least favorite subjects were next: science and mathematics.

"I'll see you after school," Riley said, planting a quick kiss on my lips as we stood near the entrance to B wing. "Gotta go get changed for gym."

"Lucky you. I'll be lucky if I don't doze off this afternoon. I wish lunch could last the rest of the day."

"Wanna go for a swim after school?"

"Sure. But this time I'll get into my swimsuit first." I smiled, kissed him again, and then watched him disappear round the corner. I checked my watch. Two minutes left of freedom. It wasn't worth going to find my sisters or friends, might as well head inside. I stepped into the corridor and blinked. The fluorescent light strips on the ceiling buzzed and glared as I walked toward the science lab. I blinked again. My eyes warmed, and each blink stung. *Oh no, not again.* I dashed into the girls' bathroom and splashed water in my eyes. No relief. Only one thing would stop it. I went to take my phone from my bag to text my sisters, when the door flung open and Serena and Talia barged in, followed by Sasha and Tamara.

"We meet again," Sasha said. "Let's get this over with." She held out her hands, and I grabbed one of them, my other hand taking hold of Serena's once she removed it from her ear.

A jolt. Bubbles. The usual.

Similar to the other fire vision we'd had, flames grew to life, flicking and curling in one giant chaotic mess. A trail of flames ran along a corridor, as though it was primed with kerosene or something. There was no stopping it. *C'mon, c'mon, give me something more! Show me something I can recognize! Where is the fire? Who lit it? C'mon!*

A buzzer sounded. *Huh?* Now I was hearing things in my visions? It buzzed again, and Serena's grip on my hand released.

"Agh! Is that a fire alarm? Is the fire here?" Serena dashed to the door, but Talia grabbed her arm.

"It's just the school bell, that's all. Lunch is over."

"But it sounded like…oh, right." Serena rubbed her ears. "Well, I heard a fire alarm in my vision, and then I thought it was really happening." She trembled, and Talia put an arm around her shoulder.

"All I saw was flames, big ones. Should we try again?" I held out my hands.

"No, let's try after school. I don't want to be late for science," Serena said, and I sighed.

With my eye pain gone, I walked with her to the lab, mentally gearing up for two hours of educational hell.

• • •

"Are you sure your sisters don't hate me?" Riley asked, eyeing the four girls walking much faster than usual ahead of us.

"No, they don't hate you. They're probably just trying to give us some privacy." *And trying to get home ASAP to connect again.*

I tightened my grip on my—check this out—*boyfriend's* hand and swung it back and forth.

"In that case, let's make the most of it." A cheeky smile slid into his cheeks, and he stopped, leaning over and giving me something even better than chocolate. *I could get used to this.* With enough kisses to satisfy me for at least the next five minutes, six if I had the willpower, we resumed the walk home.

"So, you've given riding to school the flick?" I asked.

"For now. I'd rather walk with you." He smiled. "Unless you want to get a bike of your own? Yes, then we could race each other!"

"I'd totally win."

"No you wouldn't. I might let you win at volleyball, but cycling? That'd be pushing it."

"Nothing like a bit of healthy competition."

"Yeah, for sure." He stopped. "And nothing like this, either." His arms wrapped around me and his soft lips gently pushed against mine.

Ahhh...bliss.

"Oh, geez, get a room!" Sasha called out, and I giggled, breaking away from Riley.

"She means that purely in the nonliteral sense," Talia added.

"I'm guessing there's never a dull moment at your house." Riley cocked his head toward my sisters who had returned their gaze to where it belonged, straight ahead.

"That's an understatement," I replied, which was an understatement in itself.

We eventually made it to Roach Place, and Talia discreetly mouthed, "you coming?" when she got to the front door and turned her gaze to where I stood, halfway between Riley's house and ours.

"So, see you back out here in five?" Riley asked.

"It's obvious you don't have a sister," I said. "Not many girls can be ready in five." I grinned.

"Ten?"

I glanced at the front door where Talia stood with her arms crossed. "Actually, could we make it in about half an hour instead? I forgot I had to help Serena with something." I didn't want to start this relationship off by lying, but I couldn't exactly tell him that my sisters and I needed to hold hands and predict the future before our leisurely afternoon swim. Anyway, it wasn't really a lie, I *would* be helping Serena with something: holding hands and predicting the future. What were sisters for?

"Yeah, no worries. See you in thirty."

"Yep." I planted a quick one on his lips and went inside, my sisters already waiting in the bedroom.

"Anyone would think you two weren't going to see each other for another two months or something," Sasha said, kicking off her shoes.

"Oh, shut it. You're just jealous." I crossed my arms.

"Am not. My perfect man is out there and he'll turn up when the time is right." She crossed her arms to match.

"Enough, you guys. We have important work to do." Tamara held out her hands. "Not that I really want that burnt taste in my mouth again, but if there's going to be another fire we might have a chance of stopping this one. Let's get to it."

This time the vision didn't start with fire. I saw a packet of pills, I didn't know what they were, but I—or whoever's body I was seeing this through—tipped two out and brought them to my mouth. Then darkness for a while, then a door. Was that our front door? A hand that looked like mine, unless it wasn't, opened the door and there stood Mr. Jenkins. Maybe he was seeing if we had any sugar he could borrow. But with the store an easy walk away, I doubted it. He didn't smile, but his lips moved and I hoped Serena was sensing what he was saying, because my lip reading skills weren't up to scratch. The image warped and blurred as though it was a fresh painting and water had been tipped on it, paint running down in liquid stripes. *Boom!* Orange flames burst into action behind Mr. Jenkins, and his finger was against his lips as though telling me to shush. Then blackness, with the odd flicker of yellow dancing across my eyes. Bubbles still rose and popped inside me, and this vision felt more intense than the others, more important. Another image. *Oh no.* I wished I hadn't seen it. A newspaper with the headline:

Final fire claims eight lives.

CHAPTER 11

"Geez, how long does it take to mow the lawn anyway?" Sasha asked, peering out the window at Mr. Jenkins the following Saturday afternoon. Since the vision we'd been doing a lot of peering through the window. He must have appeared in the vision for a reason, and we had to keep an eye on him.

"He might just be a perfectionist," Serena said. "Nothing wrong with that." With science her favorite subject, Serena seemed to have a soft spot for him, despite his creepiness.

"Yeah, and he might just be an arsonist." Sasha stopped spying and flopped on the couch.

"Shh," I said, turning my head to make sure Mom couldn't hear. She was out on the patio practicing her acting. The neighbors to our left probably though she was crazy, talking to herself in the back yard, but she didn't care. Inhibition was not something Mom possessed. "We don't know if he's the arsonist, what if he's someone who gets hurt, or..." I pushed the thought from my mind before the words could follow. So I wasn't that taken with our odd neighbor, but I didn't want anyone to go and die on us.

"Are you sure you didn't hear him say anything else in the vision, Serena?" Sasha asked.

"No. Like I said before, it was muffled at first, all I could make out was: 'I can take you there.'"

"Where? Where did he mean?" Sasha seemed to ask only herself. "And you heard nothing else but a crowd of people chattering, and that fire alarm?"

"That's all."

"So we don't have any specific information about where or when this is supposed to happen, all we know is it's big, it may have something to do with Mr. Jenkins, and that, um..."

"Don't say it, Talia." Serena covered her ears and her bottom lip quivered.

Eight people were going to die if we didn't stop it.

Forget homework, exams, and career options, this pressure building inside us was enough to spontaneously combust into a fire of our own. I closed my eyes and forced myself to remember the vision I'd had of the newspaper headline, to see if I could get any clues. The date on the newspaper wasn't visible, only those five awful words. If only there was a way to download our visions and store them on computer for later viewing, we might be able to analyze them better. Hang on. *Final fire claims eight lives. Final fire.* How did they know it would be the final fire? Unless...

"Guys, if the newspaper said it was the final fire, then that might mean..." I drew a deep breath, "the arsonist could be one of the eight victims, and they knew who it was."

"A small victory, then."

"Sasha!" Serena exclaimed. "It may be a good thing to

put a stop to more fires, but it's no victory for a life—for *eight* lives—to be taken away!" Tears dropped from her eyes.

"I didn't mean it like that!" She flung her hands in the air.

"Sometimes you have no heart, Sasha." Serena's voice was loose with emotion. "And what if *we* were included in those eight people, did you stop to think about that?"

"Girls, stop it! If we're going to have a chance at doing anything, we need to work together. We need to get along, so quit fighting and get your acts together." Talia stood with hands on the hips of her white cheesecloth skirt, and Serena wiped her tears.

I glanced toward the patio, Mom making enthusiastic hand gestures and speaking to an audience of garden vegetables, oblivious to our intense discussion. "We've analyzed every clue we received, there's nothing more we can do right now. All we can do is get on with our lives as best we can and keep our senses on high alert for any more clues, and," I walked to the window, Mr. Jenkins having finally finished his grass cutting, "keep a close eye on you-know-who."

"You're right." Tamara stood. "I'm hungry, who wants some pancakes?" She walked toward the kitchen.

"Me, please." Sasha followed.

I didn't respond, my eyes had just caught sight of my beloved Volleyball Guy, wearing his Video Village uniform and locking his front door. I had to get out of the house and clear my head, and what better way to do it than being with Riley, even if only for a few minutes. "Mom, I'm just going to walk with Riley to work, back soon!" I said, as I poked my head out the patio door.

"Oh, can you pick up some bread?" she asked, uncannily

able to switch from actress to mother in a split second.

"Sure." I grabbed some coins from our stash near the telephone and dashed out the front, catching up to Riley. "Want some company on your way to work?"

He turned around, a smile growing on his face. "Hey stranger, sounds good." He hooked his arm over my shoulder and we walked in time together. "Wish I didn't have to work, Saturday night was made for fun, not work." He pouted, and I leaned into his side. "But, I gotta make the cash so I can take you out to fancy places sometime." He winked.

"Aw, that's nice, but I don't need no fancy places, you know that."

"Ah, what a relief." He tipped his head back, and I flicked my hand on his chest.

"Do you mean to say that if I *did* want to go to fancy places it would be a pain in the ass?"

He raised his hands. "Hey, did I say that?"

I laughed. "I'm kidding, I don't need a fancy place to have a good time, especially with you."

"Oh, that reminds me." He clicked his fingers. "My brother's going to that indoor rock-climbing place in Fern Ridge next Sunday. He can drive us both if you want to go?"

That's the place Wayne had mentioned, maybe I'd see him there. "Awesome, I'd love to."

We walked in silence for a bit and then both spoke at the same time: "I bet I get to the top faster than you," "I'll beat you to the top."

We laughed. "How about we just have fun this time, no competition involved?" I held out my hand.

He shook it. "Deal."

Several minutes later I waved him good-bye as he served

his first customer in the video store for the afternoon; the girl from my science class with the multi-colored fingernails, whose name I now knew as Lara. She managed a brief smile, and I reciprocated. I stepped outside and turned in the direction of the store to pick up some bread. All the people on the sidewalk were walking in one of two directions, except one man up ahead, his hair graying at the sides and his hands in his pockets. He stood completely still with his eyes fixed firmly on me. My muscles clenched as I walked nearer, self-conscious to have someone's gaze on me for that long. Was he some kind of freak? Some perv? I looked away, but as I reached him he spoke.

"It was an accident."

I stopped, raised my hand above my eyes to shade them from the sun's glare. "Excuse me?"

"It was an accident. Tell him. Tell Riley."

"What was an accident? Riley's back there, in the video store." I pointed my thumb behind my shoulder.

"Tell him, please."

"But... what do you... why..." The sentence broke apart as it left my voice box, and I squinted, from the sun or confusion I didn't know. There was something different, something *strange*, about the man. *What is it?* I glanced around at people walking past us, their elongated shadows trailing behind them on the sidewalk. Then it hit me like Riley's volleyball to the head.

The man had no shadow.

• • •

I pushed through the front door and dashed toward my bedroom, grabbing the laptop out of Serena's hands on the way.

"Hey!" she said, following me. "Why'd you do that? I was researching about the genetic predisposition to psychic ability. There's definitely a clear familial link, did you know that?"

"Shh! Give me a minute." My breaths came short, sharp, and fast, and my heart pounded inside my chest.

"What are you doing?" Sasha was sitting on the floor, painting her toenails purple, a high energy song blaring from her iPod, which explained why Serena had been sitting in the living room away from the *awful noise*.

I ignored her as I typed into Google. I frantically scrolled through the search results, my eyes stretched wide. I clicked on a few results, then another. *Bingo.*

"Savvy, what's going on?" Talia and Tamara came in, and Sasha turned her music off.

The image on the screen both freaked me out and fascinated me, and this image wasn't in a vision, it was here, right in front of me, right now. My sisters, barring Sasha, peered at the screen and I pointed, my hands shaking.

"Who is that?" Talia peered closer.

I gulped. "I saw him, I saw him today."

"Robert Pearce," Talia read the name under the photo accompanying the news article about the car accident. "Hey, isn't that Riley's dad? Didn't he die?"

I nodded.

"Huh? Do you mean he's alive?" Talia's mouth gaped.

"No, he's not." I looked up from the screen to face my sister and a cold chill ran through me. "I think I just saw his ghost." The words came out as a whisper, afraid if *he* heard me he'd appear out of nowhere and scare the living daylights outta me.

Serena gasped, and Talia froze. Sasha spilt the nail polish and swore, scrambling to get up. "Are you serious?" Sasha nudged Talia out of the way to look at the picture, and Tamara sat on the bed behind me, gripping my shoulders.

"Dead serious." Oh wow, were my abilities somehow growing? I'd thought we all needed to be together for it to work, and maybe we still did, to see the future at least. But this, this was something else, this wasn't a prediction, this was a message. "And I could hear him. Not like in our visions where I can only see things, he was in front of me talking like any other person. But, oh my God, he didn't have a shadow!" I brought my trembling hands to my face, covering my eyes. "He said to tell Riley it was an accident. I didn't know what he was talking about at first, I was too confused about what I was seeing, but do you think he meant that his death was an accident?"

"Well, how did he die?" Talia asked, and I remembered I hadn't told them what Riley had revealed in confidence to me that day on the beach.

"I wasn't going to say anything, but I have to now. Riley said his father killed himself by driving off a cliff. His wife had died earlier, he was depressed, things were bad at home." I pointed to the article and they read it. My eyes tingled, the light in the room brightened, and I kept seeing Mr. Pearce's face in my mind.

"My hands are itchy," said Talia, scratching them.

"I can taste something weird, metallic." Tamara licked her lips.

"I think he wants us to connect. Maybe we'll find out the truth." I stood and held out my hands, desperate for my sisters to hold them and stop them shaking.

"But we've only ever seen the future, not the past." Serena squinted.

"Yeah, and until this day I'd never seen a ghost before. C'mon, hands out."

The door opened. "Oh, you are back, Savvy," said Mom.

Damn it, Mom! Could it be any worse a time?

"Did you get the bread?"

Crap. "I forgot, sorry, Mom, I'll go back in a minute. I just need to —"

"We're in the middle of a very important teenage girl discussion, Mom, can we have some privacy please?" Sasha batted her eyelids and flashed an 'everything is all right' smile.

"Oh, Savvy, your mind must be completely occupied by that boy of yours." She sighed. "Teenage hormones... ah, those were the days."

"Mom?" Sasha raised her eyebrows.

"Oh, right. I'll leave you to it, then. And don't worry, I'll get the bread myself." She closed the door. "Back in fifteen!" she called from the hallway, the front door banging a moment later.

"Quick, quick! This light is too much!" I shut my eyes and grasped hold of my nearest two sisters, and my body shuddered from the jolt.

All sound faded, my body numbed, and my sight was the only sense I had. This time, it was like a movie. I wasn't in the body of a person, I was watching them. Riley's dad sat in the driver's seat, hands resting comfortably on the steering wheel, his eyes focused on the road ahead. I really didn't want to see this, but I had to. The car was tilted forward a little, the road inclining, and there were trees and bushland all around. From what the news article had said, his car had gone off a cliff about a half hour away from Iris Harbor, not far from a popular lookout that had one hundred and eighty degree views, and overlooked a deep valley. His face was pale with dark shadows under his eyes, but he didn't appear to be in any sort of disturbed state. What would someone look like if they were about to launch off a cliff on purpose? Then something strange happened... right when his hands veered the steering wheel slightly to the left to go around the bend, his left hand went limp and fell from the wheel. His head flopped to the left as well, like he was having a stroke, and his right hand tried to maneuver the wheel on its own to compensate. It didn't work, the car didn't move with the bend in the road. It kept going straight, and pushed through the silver barrier on the side of the road, becoming airborne until it crashed and tumbled down the embankment and landed in a crumpled, twisted heap in the valley below. I didn't see him after that, didn't need to. The wreckage told me all I needed to know, and what I'd seen in the moments before told me exactly what he'd told me himself: It was, without a doubt, an accident.

"No!" Talia screamed, as we released our hands. "Oh my God!" She hugged her arms around her body, shaking.

I panted, covered my eyes, and crumbled to the floor. "I can't handle this!"

"I don't ever want to hear that sound again," Serena said, wrapping her arms around Talia, who would have felt what Robert Pearce had felt, at least to some degree. Sasha and Tamara were less affected by their slighter senses, and they hooked their arms under mine and helped me stand.

Talia sobbed. "The pain, oh my God, the pain!" She curled in on herself and Serena patted her back. "Before it happened," she sniffed, "My whole left side felt numb. I could feel my right hand trying to control the wheel, my brain urging my left hand to lift up and take control, but it was paralyzed. I couldn't do anything. I felt weightless for a few seconds, and then the most jarring, sudden crashing against my body. It was like nothing I've ever experienced." She broke down again and I held onto her arm. We stood there, hugging together like one body, crying and sniffing, and wishing like mad we hadn't had to experience that.

After a few minutes I broke away and wiped my tears with the back of my hand. "I have to tell him. I have to tell Riley." My voice shook.

"No!" Talia said. "He doesn't need to know about this, I wouldn't want anyone to know what this was like."

"But he thinks his dad took his own life. He hates him for it!"

"Savvy, you can't just rock up to his place and say, *hey, I saw your dad's ghost and then he gave me a vision of the day he died and it wasn't suicide*," Sasha said. "He won't believe you, and he'll think we're all freaks!"

"How can you be so selfish and worry what he thinks of us?" Serena cried. "I agree with Savannah. He deserves to know the truth. Wouldn't you want to know the truth about our dad if someone knew it?"

"If I hadn't have experienced... this, I wouldn't believe them. And I seriously doubt Riley would believe us. Besides, Savvy, do you really want to risk your relationship with him?"

No, I didn't. But how could I be with him and act

normal, knowing what I know now?

"Okay, okay, let's think rationally," Tamara said, pushing her palms downward as if to quash the rising tension. "We know the truth now, but yesterday we didn't. Riley, and his brother for that matter, are going about their business as usual and by the looks of things are doing okay. Not perfect, but okay. If we rock the boat, it may make things worse if they don't believe us. Savvy," she turned to face me, "I think you should keep things the way they are, enjoy your time with him, and just suss things out a bit. Get into a conversation about, um...*supernatural* stuff and see what his beliefs are. Then you can reassess whether to tell him or not. But don't do it without getting our agreement first, okay? This affects all of us."

I nodded. "Okay. I'll suss things out first."

"I still don't think you should tell him." Sasha crossed her arms.

Tamara looked at her. "Let's just take it one day at a time, okay?"

I slowed my breathing, tried to get back to some sort of normalcy, and a surprising flicker of hope sparked inside. "Hey, if I can see ghosts, but I haven't seen Dad, then maybe he's still alive! You'd think if I was going to see who I needed to see, he'd show himself, right? He'd let us know so we could stop wondering, put him to rest, and move on. But I haven't seen him." I straightened my posture. "He could still be alive."

CHAPTER 12

That little flicker of hope, that floating ember of possibility, kept me going. It was also keeping my mind off the fact that I hadn't passed on Robert Pearce's message to his son. How could I? I wanted to, deep inside, *really* wanted to, but it could go one of two ways: he'd thank me profusely and think it was pretty awesome that I had such an amazing gift, or he'd think I was lying, deluded, crazy—or all three—and never want to see me again. Something told me it would most likely be the latter, and I didn't want to risk losing what we had together. Was that selfish? Or should I cast my own wants and needs aside in order to honor the truth? The pros and cons swung back and forth inside me. One moment I'd be convinced I could never tell him, then I'd swing the other way and change my mind.

At least I'd forgotten about my dilemma for an hour or so this afternoon as we'd rock-climbed—the *fake* plastic rock-climbing that is—along with Riley's brother, Leo. Mom's Knight in shining armor hadn't been there, but I hadn't expected him to be; the play wasn't far off and I was sure he'd be at the extra Sunday rehearsal helping Mom out.

Leo had dropped us back home and gone off to visit a friend, leaving us alone at his house. *One bonus of not having parents around, I guess.* As I sat with Riley on the couch in his living room, credits rolling on the movie we'd just watched, his lips rolled gently across mine.

Mmm... I hope these credits last as long as... as long as... which movies have never-ending credits? Harry Potter? Lord of the Rings? Ah, who cares!

My hands slipped around his back as his ran through my hair, pulling me closer. My eyes opened a fraction as the light sneaking between the venetian blinds behind Riley twinkled. My lips separated from Riley's as I giggled.

"What's so funny?" He smiled.

I raised my chin in the direction of the side table underneath the window and he turned to look. "Oh man, I'm so used to those photos being there I forgot to hide them from you!"

"I'm glad you didn't. You were a cute baby." I pinched his cheeks then walked up to the photos displayed on the table. I picked up one of him and his brother nestled in their mother's arms. A wave of sadness rolled through me. No child should ever have to lose a parent so young, let alone two. I narrowed my eyes as I glanced at the other photos, then around the walls of the living room. "There aren't any photos of..." I cleared my throat "...your father?"

Riley stood and shoved his hands into his pockets. "Took 'em down."

"Oh."

"I don't want to be reminded of what he did." He

straightened the cushions on the couch that had fallen askew from our snuggling together.

The pendulum. *There it goes again.*

I placed the photo down and my fingers threaded together, twisting and turning around in indecision, much like my insides. "So, um, did your dad leave a... note or anything?"

Riley's eyes connected with mine. "A suicide note? Nope. Didn't even have the decency."

"Have you, um..." I twisted my hands even more "... ever considered the possibility that it might have been an accident?" The last word came out as a whisper.

Riley's eyes shot wide open. "What?" He stepped closer. "I told you what happened. He drove off a cliff, not far from..."

"Far from where?"

"From the lookout at Fern Ridge. He used to take Mom there sometimes, even proposed to her there. He'd gone there that day one last time, and obviously didn't want to return home."

I shivered as I remembered the steep cliff hanging off the bend we'd driven around on our way back from the rock-climbing center. I thought it had looked familiar, from what I'd seen in my vision. And both Riley and Leo had gone dead quiet for a minute as Leo drove extra slowly around the bend. I was surprised they could even be there, knowing that's where their father took his last breath.

Is my father still breathing? I drew a deep breath and hoped that the same air filling my lungs was filling his too. Somewhere.

"So you don't think he could have just been upset and

not concentrating on the road, or —"

"No. He was a good driver. He may have been depressed but he wasn't stupid." Riley paced up and down the room. "Oh, he knew what he was doing, all right. He preferred the idea, the *hope*, of being reunited with Mom in some other place rather than being with us. He made his choice."

Reunited. Some other place...

"Do you think, I mean, do you believe in that stuff? In life after death?"

Riley shrugged, scratched his head. "Maybe. I dunno. Who knows? The only thing I do believe right now is that Dad chose his own needs over those of his children."

I bit my lip. I willed the pendulum to swing back to the other side, but it hung there on one side; strong, stubborn, as though Robert Pearce was holding it in place with his bare hands. *'Tell him,'* the memory of his voice whispered in my ear.

My legs weakened and I sat on the couch, the anger and disappointment in Riley's voice pushing the truth toward my voice box. I swallowed, gulped, tried to push it back down, but my lips parted and words came out. "Riley, I have to tell you something."

He stopped in front of me. "What is it?"

"Sit down." I tugged on his arm.

"Whenever anyone says 'sit down' it usually means bad news."

"It's not. I mean, not really. It's just..." I took another deep breath and willed my heart to slow down. "You may not believe what I'm about to say, but please hear me out."

Creases formed in Riley's forehead.

Where do I start?

"Remember how I told you I was in a coma?"

He nodded. "Is something wrong, are you sick again?" He placed his hand on my arm.

"Hell, no." I placed my hand on top of his, touched by his concern, but also worried I may never get the chance to touch his hand again. "When I woke up, something happened. Something... out of the ordinary. I started to be able to, um, see certain things, more clearly."

Riley's forehead creases deepened.

C'mon, Savannah, just tell him.

"My sisters and I, together, we can see things, *sense* things. Things that are going to happen. And sometimes..." *well, once,* "...things that *have* happened. Like that liquor store fire. We had a vision of it before it happened."

Riley's concerned face softened and he threw his head back with a laugh. "Ah, good one. Is it April Fool's Day already?"

"Riley. I'm serious. I've seen things. And I've seen..."

Here goes nothing.

"Riley, I've seen your dad."

He removed his hand and stood. "What are you talking about? He's dead."

"I know he's dead. But he's still... *here.* He came to me, told me to tell you that his death was an accident."

Riley stepped backward, ran a heavy hand through his hair and rested it on the back of his neck.

"I know it's hard to believe, but please. Believe me. I had a vision of the day he died, I saw what he saw. He—"

"Get out!" Riley yelled, his finger pointing sharply at the door. I stood with a jolt, and made the mistake of approaching him. He pushed my arms away as I held them out to him. "Why? Why would you do this? Are you playing a cruel trick or do you have some deluded belief that what you're saying is true?" His hands flailed about wildly as he spoke.

"It's no trick. It's true. I didn't want to tell you but when I discovered the truth about your dad, I just had to!" Tears welled in my eyes. "Riley, please. Please believe me. Your dad wanted you to know that he didn't take his own life. You need to know the truth!"

He laughed and shook his head. "Geez, that coma must have messed with your mind." He twirled his finger in circles beside his head, and then his expression turned serious. "I was wrong to get involved with you. You and your sisters are nothing but a bunch of freaks. Go, get out!"

My bottom lip trembled, my heart sunk, and tears spilled from my eyes. I turned away and flung open the front door, dashing outside and barging into my house. I went straight to the bedroom and collapsed on the bed.

"Savvy, what's wrong?" Serena asked, sitting next to me and placing her hand on my back as I sobbed. I turned to face her, and Sasha bolted into the room.

Realization dawned in Sasha's eyes. "Oh, no, Savannah. What have you done?"

CHAPTER 13

"What about you, Savvy, would you like to watch TV with us?" Mom asked as she sat comfortably next to Wayne on the couch. The new heart-shaped necklace he'd given her glinted in the light.

I pointed listlessly to the bag of garbage waiting by the front door. "No, it's okay. I'll just, um, go on the computer after I put this out."

"You girls don't seem to watch much TV lately, which I guess is a good thing. You spend an awful lot of time in that bedroom," Mom commented. "Still, at least you all seem to be getting along most of the time. I can't complain about that."

"Yeah, well there's a lot more homework now too; it's quicker if we help each other." That was true of course, but not the whole reason we spent so much time in the bedroom.

"Well, it sounds like you're being very efficient. I'm proud of you, sweetheart." Mom blew a kiss.

"Thanks, Mom." I scratched behind my ear. Homework

was the last thing on my mind lately, especially the last few days after my breakup with Riley. On Monday he'd avoided me like I was infected with some deadly virus; and for the last three days, he hadn't been at school at all. Had our argument upset him enough to avoid going to school? Or maybe he was just sick. I kept my eyes on the window, but his blinds were usually closed; and I had no idea what he was thinking or if he'd told anyone about my secret. *Our* secret. We hadn't been subjected to any teasing or bullying, so with any luck he'd kept his mouth shut. How long that would last, I didn't know.

"You waiting for him, love?" Mom asked with a knowing look on her face.

I shrugged.

"You sure you don't want to talk about why you broke up? It seemed to be going so well."

"Yeah," Wayne added. "I can leave you two alone if you like. I don't want to get in the way."

"No, it's fine." I crossed my arms.

"You sure he didn't treat you badly or anything, because if he did, I swear I'll—"

"No, Mom. He didn't. It's nothing, don't worry."

"Okay, but I'm here if you need me."

I nodded and kept watch for another few minutes, until Riley's front door opened. The sun was fading, but he didn't put his porch light on, as though he didn't want to attract my attention. Well that didn't work. I could still see, could even see things with my eyes *closed*, not that he believed me.

Riley walked over to his garbage can and dumped the bags inside it, and then wheeled it to the curb as I dashed outside with garbage bag in hand. "Are you stalking me or something?" he asked, irritation lining his face.

"I'm just putting out the garbage like you are," I replied, dumping the bag in the can.

"Yeah, right." He shook his head and made an annoyed "tsk" sound.

"Riley. When are you going to listen to what I have to say? There are things I need to explain. You might not believe me, but at least let me finish what I was trying to tell you the other day. I'm not wacko; I'm just trying to help." I held up my palms in desperation.

"You've said enough. Enough for me to know I don't want you anywhere near me or my brother." He turned away, and then turned back and flicked his hand at me. "Go back to your crystal ball and leave me the hell alone."

He slammed his door closed and left me standing there on the side of the road. Helpless. Alone. An outcast.

With heavy shoulders, I staggered back into the house and ignored the curious eyes of Wayne and Mom. I don't think I exhaled until I reached the soft comfort of my bed.

"Didn't go well, I take it?" Sasha asked.

"What do *you* think?"

"What *I* think," Serena piped up, "is that if he's not prepared to accept you the way you are then he's not worth it."

"But we got along so well." I buried my face in my pillow. "I wish he would have believed me."

"There's nothing more you could have done. You can't make him believe. Unless…" Serena tapped her chin. "Did his dad give you any information or signs that Riley would recognize? Something specific that only he would know?"

"You mean proof," said Sasha.

"Yeah. If you can prove it to him, then he has to believe you."

I racked my brain and searched my memory of that terrible vision. Nothing. All I knew was what happened to him and what he looked like, but I could have easily looked that up on the Internet. "Nope. If only he'd reappear and give me some other way of getting through to Riley."

Was I really asking for a ghost to come back and scare the crap out of me? *I must be losing it.*

"Let's connect." Serena tugged on my hand.

"I didn't mean right *now*." I pulled my hand away.

"There's no time like the present," she said, and Sasha agreed.

"Not tonight." I sighed. "I'm tired."

"You okay?" asked Talia. "No headaches or anything?"

I sat up and crossed my arms. "No. No headaches, no dizziness, no blurred vision, and no aneurysm!" Why did they overreact to every little thing?

"Savvy—"

I held up my hand. "I don't want to discuss it." I looked at my sisters' concerned faces and sighed. "Oh, all right. Let's get this over with." I held out my hands.

The jolt still surprised me, even though it was expected. A bit like when toast pops up in the toaster—you know it's going to, but it still makes you jump. The bubbly sensation was more appealing, light and floaty, energizing; but as for what came after, well, that depended on what I'd see.

And what I saw took my breath away. *Was I really seeing this? Could it be?*

Serena's hand slipped from mine and I opened my eyes.

"Dad?" she whispered. "I think I heard Dad's voice."

"I *saw* him." Hope rose inside me. "I saw him! Does this mean we're going to see him again in real life? In the future?" My nerves jumped and jiggled. I could barely contain them.

"His aftershave, I could smell it," said Sasha. "Not that I remember what it was, I just knew somehow it was his."

"Could it have been him from the past, not the future?" Talia asked. "What did he look like, Savvy? Savvy?"

My heart rate doubled in speed. "Like that," I whispered, pointing out the window. I walked over and rested my hands on the glass pane. "Dad?"

It was him. Right outside my window! *He's here, he's back, he's...*

"Like what?" Talia asked. "What are you looking at?" Her gaze followed mine.

"Y...you can't...see him?" My voice shook. "But—"

"Savvy, there's no one there."

I glanced at my sisters, my eyes urging them to see what I saw. Their confused expressions told me they didn't.

"It's Dad! Dad's standing right there!" I jabbed my finger toward him, and then wound the window open as fast as I could, pushing the glass pane outward at an angle. "Dad!" I leaned out. "Dad!"

He smiled and waved, but his expression was distant, sad, resigned.

Tears spilled from my eyes as he walked closer to the window. I turned to my sisters and my chin quivered. "He's there, don't you see him?" They shook their heads.

No. No, it couldn't be. He couldn't be.

He's...dead?

"My darling, Savannah," he said, and my breath caught in my throat. "I didn't want you to see me like this." He turned his head to the side.

"Dad, what happened to you? When? Why? How?" A million unanswered questions ran through my mind and scrambled over each other for attention.

"Savvy, you must stay away from him," he said, as though he hadn't heard my question, my desperate plea to find out what happened to him. "All of you; stay away from him." His body faded slightly, and I could see the background through him; he was partly transparent. "I can't stay long, it's hard for me, I don't know how…" He dissolved away and came back again like bad reception on an old television. The sun was gone, but the moon shone, yet still there was no shadow to be seen; no evidence of life in my father's body. It was just a remnant, a faded image of who he once was. "It's not fair." He covered his eyes with his hand, shielding his sadness. "It should be me in there with her." He shook his head, lowering his chin to his chest.

"Dad, look at me. Tell me what happened."

He raised his head. "He watches. He watches you all. Stay away, please."

"Who, Dad? Who?"

"The one who plays with fire. The flames, he needs them. He needs to keep the fire burning. For her. For the one he lost." His chin lowered to his chest, and his image faded till I could barely see him. "Don't let her forget me," he whispered, and then his body reappeared as clear as if he was really standing outside my window. "It's up to you now, Savvy. You have to stop it."

I wanted to climb out the window and fling my arms around him, but I knew I couldn't touch him, could never feel the comfort of his arms around me, could never feel his love and protection. "Dad?" His name had barely left my mouth when he disappeared. Gone. Again. "No!"

I flinched as hands gripped my shoulders and pulled me backward.

"Savannah, come and sit down." Talia led me toward the bed, my eyes not wanting to look away from the now empty front yard.

The reality of what I'd just seen hit me like a shot of adrenaline to the heart. "It's over," I said. "There's no more hope. He's gone. Dad's really gone." My face dropped to my hands and tears dripped through my fingers. "Dad's dead!" My body shuddered and shook with sadness as my sisters embraced me and we wrapped and tangled in each other in one big clump of grief.

"You really saw him?" Serena asked, her voice shaking. "His...ghost?"

"Yes," I cried. "Just like Riley's dad."

"And you heard him too? But...I didn't. How, why..." Serena's body matched the trembling of her voice.

We hugged and sobbed, and his words ran through my mind, all jumbled up. I couldn't make sense of them now, didn't have room for them. My whole being was completely overtaken with unrelenting grief, with sickening sadness, anger, and the horrible, horrible truth that my father had succumbed to the outcome we most feared.

I unwrapped myself from my sisters arms and stood. "I have to tell Mom. She needs to know." Without waiting for my sisters' agreement or objection, I dashed out of the bedroom and into a reality that was worse than my coma.

CHAPTER 14

"Mom." My voice quivered and tears streamed down my face.

"Savvy, what is it?" Mom shot up. "Oh, sweetheart, is this about Riley? Come here, let's talk about it." She held out her arms.

"It's not about him, it's worse."

Wayne checked his watch. "I, ah, better get going. It's getting late." He pecked Mom's cheek and grabbed his wallet and keys from the mantle above the converted bookcase.

Mom mouthed "sorry" to him and escorted him to the door.

"Come and sit down; tell me what's going on." I sat next to Mom, and my sisters emerged glossy-eyed from the bedroom. "Oh no, you're all upset? Have you been arguing? What is it?"

I held my hand up to tell my sisters that I had it under control, that I'd take charge of breaking the news. After all, I was the only one who had seen him. But first, I'd have to break the other news; the news that we had a gift. Otherwise, how would she ever comprehend the fact that I'd seen Dad?

Talia and Tamara sat next to me on the couch, and Serena sat on the armchair twisting the hem of her top into a knot while Sasha perched on its arm.

Her face creased with concern, Mom took a deep breath. "It's not, I mean, you haven't had any…symptoms return, have you?"

"No, Mom, no. I'm fine. It's not that."

She exhaled and her shoulders relaxed.

"Mom, do you believe in the afterlife?"

Her eyes widened and she fiddled with her new necklace. "The afterlife? What's brought this on?"

"Do you?" I urged.

She glanced at my sisters, whose faces remained fixed on Mom's. "Well, as a matter of fact, I do."

The breath that had been caught in my throat released. One hurdle dealt with, another two to go.

"I believe our souls go on to a better place after we die. Why do you ask?"

"And do you believe that some people can *communicate* with those who've crossed over, or even sense things that are going to happen in the future?" I never thought I'd have this conversation with my mother, ever. Talia, maybe, but not me. Talia hadn't even considered bringing out the Ouija board for a while. I think it freaked her out now that she knew all this stuff was real. But who needed one anyway when I was practically a human Ouija board?

Mom gulped and patted down her skirt, and then fiddled with the hem. "Um, well, if people's spirits live on after they die then it's possible that some people could be able to sense their presence."

"And see the future?"

Mom shrugged. "And see the future, sure, why not?"

I knew Mom was pretty open-minded and a bit new agey and all that, but this was going better than expected. Then again, I hadn't got to the bad news yet.

"Why the sudden interest?" Mom's eyebrows drew together. "Have you been reading things on the Internet? Have you been playing around with that silly Ouija board?"

"No," I replied, and then took her hand in mine. "Mom, ever since my coma, my senses have been heightened. I've been able to...*see* certain things."

Her hand trembled in mine then gripped it harder.

"Some of the things I've seen have come true. But it's not just me; we've all experienced things." I gestured to my sisters. "Except, each of us is gifted with only one of the five senses. I know it sounds crazy, and we were afraid to tell you, but please believe us."

My sisters nodded as Mom's eyes silently asked for confirmation of the truth.

"So, you get visions or something?" She resumed fiddling with her necklace, sliding it between her thumb and forefinger.

I nodded. "But only when we're all together. We just kinda hold hands and it happens. Then we try to put all the senses together to make sense of it."

"Oh my God." Mom's eyes appeared to be lost in some other world, and then she looked at me again. "So that's why you've been hanging out together so much, locked away in that bedroom?"

We nodded.

She shook her head in amazement. "Well, what have you seen?"

Sasha shifted on the armrest and Talia cleared her throat.

"A few insignificant things, and a few important things," I said, noticing my tears had dried up and my voice was now strong and calm. Maybe it was the relief in getting all of this out in the open. "That fire in town, we saw it before it happened, only we didn't know where it was going to be or when."

Mom's hand flew to her mouth.

"And recently, I saw something all on my own, without everyone being together. It wasn't a vision. It was a person, a..."

"Ghost?" Mom said the word that I couldn't, her eyes wide open.

I nodded. "Riley's dad. That's why we broke up. I told him and he didn't believe me."

Mom caressed my cheek. "Oh dear, I'm so sorry. What did his dad want?"

"So, you actually believe me? You believe that I saw a ghost?" Could my mom be the best mom ever?

"You're my daughter, of course I believe you. I didn't raise you to be dishonest. If you believe you've seen something, then I believe you."

I glanced at Talia and Tamara, who had both relief and dread in their faces, if that was even possible. Relief at having Mom on our side and dread that she didn't yet know what we knew.

"He wanted me to tell Riley that his death wasn't suicide as everyone had thought. It was an accident. Mom, I saw what he saw. I saw his father's death." My tears returned, welling up in my eyes, but determined not to spill until I'd managed to get everything out in the open. "I think he had a stroke. He lost the ability to move on one side, and the car went over the cliff. It was awful."

Tears welled in Mom's eyes too, and she pulled me in close to her body. I pulled back. If I stayed there I might not want to leave. I might cry and never stop. I might not be able to tell her about Dad.

"Riley wouldn't let me go into detail, so he still doesn't know the truth. He hates his dad for leaving him behind. And I hate that I know what really happened, but the one person who needs to know won't listen."

Mom rubbed her hand up and down my back. "Give it time, love. Maybe he'll find out on his own."

How? Unless by some miracle he started seeing ghosts himself; or, even more unlikely, listened to me and believed what I said.

"So all this has got you upset and confused, huh?" She continued rubbing my back.

If only that was all.

I straightened my back and sat tall. "That's not all, Mom. There's something else." I was sure my heartbeat was audible as it thumped fast inside me like a drumroll. "I saw another ghost," I whispered. "Just before."

My eyes must have somehow revealed the identity of the ghost, because Mom's bottom lip quivered and she stood, stepping backward. She shook her head. "No, no, no." Her hands ran through her hair and her eyes pleaded with mine. "Don't tell me, no."

I stood and inched toward her, giving a slight but definite nod. She backed up against the wall, her body trembling, and then sunk to the floor in a sobbing heap. "Oh, David, no! Not you, no!"

I sat next to her on the floor and held her in my arms. My mother. The one who'd held me after my diagnosis. The one who'd stayed by my side until I woke from the coma. The one who'd helped me through my recovery and comforted me when I was overwhelmed. I was in pain too, but it was nothing compared to the loss my mom felt. He'd been her husband, her soulmate, her best friend. Now the hope was gone. *He* was gone, for good.

My sisters joined the embrace and like we'd done in the privacy of our room, we sat there together, united in grief.

When Mom's sobs turned to sniffles she asked, "What did he say, Savannah? Did he talk to you?"

I wiped my face with the back of my hand and nodded. "He wasn't one hundred percent clear, and he didn't say what happened to him. All he was concerned with was us staying away from someone. But he didn't give a name, just said we all had to stay away from *him*. That *he* was watching us, and that I had to stop it. I think he meant the arsonist, whoever that might be. He also—"

"Also what?"

"I could be wrong, but I think he was feeling a bit…I dunno, jealous might be too strong a word. He said it should have been him in here with you instead of Wayne."

Mom clamped her lips together then spoke. "Why now? Why, just when I'm moving on with my life and things are looking up, is this happening? It's not fair!" She buried her face in her hands. "It took me years to even consider moving on from David, and the moment I do, he goes and shows himself, and not in the way I would have hoped."

"Mom, you didn't do anything wrong by moving on, it's been nine years," said Talia. "I'm sure Dad would just want you to be happy."

"By the sounds of it he doesn't want me to move on, though. Could he really be jealous of Wayne?"

"I don't know. Maybe it's just strange for him," I said.

"Who do you think he meant for us to stay away from?" Sasha asked. "Do you think he meant Mr. Jenkins? I've seen him *watching* through his window."

That's exactly what I was thinking. But could a high school science teacher really be a criminal? Maybe Dad made an appearance to warn us about him.

"Don't take this the wrong way, Savvy, but what if he meant *Riley*."

I glared at Serena. "Why would he want me to stay away from Riley? So he doesn't believe what I—what *we*—can do, but that doesn't make him a bad person. Besides, he said all of us needed to stay away from him."

"Well, we do live across the street from him," she said.

"And Mr. Jenkins lives next door." I crossed my arms.

"But didn't Riley seem fascinated by the liquor store fire that night?" Sasha remarked.

"No, it couldn't be him." Surely not. I wouldn't believe it for a second.

"Guys, c'mon, it might not be either of them," Talia said. "What about Riley's brother?"

"Leo?" I barely knew him, but he did seem a little troubled. No wonder though, if Riley's troubles were anything to go by. Leo had become a brother and parent in one, and probably felt trapped by his responsibilities. "Oh, I don't know. Maybe Dad'll come back and be a bit more specific next time."

"They're usually quite vague," said Mom. "Especially if they're confused or traumatized by their own deaths; they might not completely understand what's happening."

I looked at Mom blankly, and then at my sisters who appeared to share my confusion. "Mom, what do you mean? How do you know?"

Her eyes caught mine and she bit her lip as though she'd been busted elbow deep in the cookie jar. "Oh dear," she said. "I was wondering if this would ever come to light." She stood, smoothing down her skirt. "Come with me, girls. There's something you need to see."

CHAPTER 15

Mom ushered us into her bedroom and my sisters and I sat on her queen-size bed. It looked strange with one lone pillow in the center; another reminder of the absence of our father. Mom moved the stool from her dressing table over to the closet and stepped on top of it. She still had to stand on tiptoes to reach the top of the closet, so I guess I had her to thank for my height challenges. She pushed aside a pile of blankets and reached toward the back, extracting a tattered shoebox. She stepped down and brought it over to us on the bed.

She eased off the lid and placed it to the side; the movement was slow and deliberate. I wanted to tip the box over and rummage through it with gusto, but Mom's hands hovered delicately over the box as though it might explode at any second.

"I...I haven't looked at these in so long," she said, her curls falling onto her face as her head tilted forward over the box. A faint smell of stale potpourri wafted from the box as Mom opened up the layer of purple satin fabric that concealed the box's contents.

No one dared speak, we simply waited. Waited for her to share whatever she was going to share. My muscles were clenched and my eyes unblinking.

She pulled out a business card and a hint of a smile crept up one corner of her mouth. "I've always been a massage therapist as you know, but back when your father was...*alive*, I used to do something else on the side, too." She held the card out in front for all of us to see. Five heads inched closer to read the small print.

Rose ~ Psychic Medium and Intuitive Counselor

Holy crap. My mom was a freaking psychic? How did we not know this?

"But, Mom, you never said—" Serena started, overshadowed by Sasha who said, "You're psychic? Why on earth didn't you tell us?"

I glanced at Talia who mouthed "no way" as she shook her head in disbelief.

Mom took the card back. "Was. I *was* psychic." She shifted on the bed and tucked her foot under her other leg. "When your father disappeared, my abilities disappeared too, for some reason. I tried and tried to make them work, wanted desperately to use them to find out what happened to him, but nothing. And nothing since. I'd almost forgotten about my past until you told me your little secret just now." She pulled out something else from the box, a candle, and brought it to her nose.

"Is that cinnamon?" Sasha asked.

Mom nodded. "And lemongrass. Heightens psychic awareness." She put it back in the box and withdrew a black stone.

"Onyx," I said, remembering Riley's recall of what he'd learned from Google about my earrings. Instinctively my hand touched my ear, also remembering his touch when he'd replaced my earring.

Mom flipped through a pile of papers and cards, opening one and bringing a hand to her heart. "These are thank you cards and letters I received from my clients."

"So you used to do readings for people and earn money for your work?" Tamara asked.

"Yes. It was mostly word of mouth, and my existing massage clients. I was careful not to expose myself too much through advertising, for the sake of you girls. I knew what I did was helpful to people, but not everyone thinks that way, unfortunately."

Don't I know it.

"What are we doing wasting time at school, girls? We could be laughing all the way to the bank!" Tamara's attempt to lighten the mood brought a few faint smiles.

"It's a big responsibility. You have to be well practiced and confident in your abilities. They can take time to develop," Mom said. "Mine began as a heightening of each sense, one at a time. At first my sense of smell became strong, then taste, then my hearing, then my hands became ultrasensitive to touch, and then…then the sights around me became clearer, brighter, more detailed. Then I started seeing things that others couldn't. My mother didn't believe me at first until I told her what Dad had said to her on their first date when they were young." Mom grinned.

"So this is hereditary?" Serena asked. "Because I've been researching."

"It can be, but not always. Though I don't know why you each got one of the five senses instead of the whole spectrum. Maybe it somehow dispersed among you. It can be triggered by a significant event in life, so Savvy waking from her coma could have brought it out."

"That's what we thought," Serena said. "We thought it might have something to do with delta brain waves?"

"Who knows?" Mom said. "I've heard about those, but I've never really been one to look into the scientific side of it. You get that from your father, Serena." Mom winked. "He always wanted to know how things worked."

"And Dad knew about your *gift?*"

Mom nodded. "That's another reason he was so great. He supported me one hundred percent." Mom's smile faded. "I just wish I'd been able to predict what happened to him. Sometimes it's a cruel gift; it shows you things you don't want to see and won't always show you what you want to see."

We nodded. "Amen to that."

"Although, I did advise him not to go ahead with leasing the premises he wanted for his computer repair store. Something wasn't right about it, but I didn't know much more than that. He took it into account, but when I failed to bring up any specific reason not to go ahead with it, he decided to take the risk anyway, and I accepted that. Considering he was last seen near the premises makes me wish he *had* taken my advice after all." A tear found its way out of Mom's eye and she wiped it away. "Oh well, no use wondering what might have been."

I wanted to ask more about Dad's disappearance and Mom's bad feeling about his store, but I didn't want to upset her any further. "Did you have to do anything specific to get visions, or did they just come to you?" I asked.

"It helps to clear the mind and take some deep breaths, but when I first realized I had a gift, I'd get little flashes of insight at random times throughout the day or night. Not to mention the odd unexpected visitor. I could be in the middle of a conversation with someone and an uninvited guest would sit down to join us, trying to get my attention. Or they'd appear behind the person, and then disappear and reappear until I couldn't concentrate and would have to find somewhere private to speak to them. I soon learned to control it a bit better, and having appointment times helped as a way of letting them know when I was 'open for business,' so to speak. Not that it worked all the time, but it at least gave some structure to the whole thing."

"Well I wish these ghosts would make an appointment with me instead of giving me such a shock." I rubbed my eyes, worn out from crying and probably from seeing. Mom's bedside lamp was on, but it seemed too bright. Sasha sniffled and Serena rubbed her ear.

Hang on. *Oh, not again!*

"Are you thinking what I'm thinking?" asked Sasha.

I nodded. "We need to connect. Mom, we're getting 'enhanced sensory perception,' as Serena calls it, and this has been happening sometimes when there's something we need to see." I stood and my sisters gathered around me.

"Do you think it's Dad trying to get through to us again?" asked Serena. "Do you see him anywhere, Savvy?"

I looked around the room and pushed aside the drapes. "Nope."

"Do you need me to leave the room while you, um…"

Mom clasped her hands awkwardly together.

"No, Mom, stay. Maybe it'll trigger something in you. Maybe you'll finally see Dad." I had no idea if that was possible, but if she'd had the gift before, surely it could return now that she had some degree of closure about Dad's disappearance?

It felt weird to be doing this around Mom, but she appeared to be kinda proud of us, yet concerned at the same time. We held hands and closed our eyes, and I hoped this vision wouldn't end in tears.

Mentally I prepared myself to see Dad. I wanted so badly for him to tell us what happened and where his body was so we could lay him to rest, but instead I saw...*myself*?

I was in someone else's point of view, watching myself go into my house. The image got smaller and I realized where I was: Riley's living room. The narrow wooden table under the front window had the same photos I'd looked at last Sunday. Come to think of it, the outfit I was wearing as I went into the house was the same one I'd worn last Sunday. Could this vision be of the past? It looked like I was in Riley's point of view, watching myself dash off after our argument.

The image changed, and my line of sight shot to the right, as though a camera had suddenly moved toward the source of a sound. It was like one of those low-budget shaky cam movies where you're seeing things through the character's eyes. I was looking down the hallway in Riley's house, and his volleyball rolled from an open doorway—probably his bedroom—and into another doorway directly opposite. I followed it, and Riley's hands picked it up from the bathroom floor and returned it to the shelf in his bedroom.

Then blackness. Now I was looking *at* Riley sitting at the kitchen table eating a bowl of pasta. Nothing exciting there, until he shivered and faint goose bumps prickled his bare arms. He rubbed them with his hands and glanced warily around the room. Blackness again. Then Riley rummaged through a cardboard box on the floor. He pulled out a photo of his dad and looked at it, pain darkening his eyes. Despite the way he'd spoken to me and dismissed my attempt to help last weekend, my heart lurched at the sight of him pushing back tears. The lights above him flickered, and he glanced up at the ceiling, his forehead creased. He shoved the photo back in the box then turned out the light, signaling the end of my vision.

"Is that it?" I asked, breaking our circle. "Nothing to do with Dad?"

"You didn't see him? Or sense him?" Mom asked, perched stiffly on the edge of the bed, her white-knuckled hands gripping the edge.

I shook my head. "All I saw was Riley."

"So that's who was digging into that delicious pasta dish?" asked Tamara. "I kind of like getting to taste things without the calories." She attempted a laugh.

"It smelled good," added Sasha, breathing in deep.

"I think this was in the past. I saw myself the day we broke up. He was watching me go back into the house."

"What else? What did you see?" asked Mom, and I wondered if now that she knew about our gift, she'd harass us every night until we revealed details of each vision. This could get to be a pain in the ass.

"I think Riley's dad was trying to communicate with him," I said. "A ball rolled off the shelf for no reason, he got cold all of a sudden at dinner, and when he was looking at a photo of his father, the lights flickered on and off. He looked a bit freaked out."

"Ah, yes. Spirits can sometimes manipulate electricity and temperature with their energy. If they're strong or they really want to get through to someone, they can also move things." Mom spoke like she was explaining something simple and ordinary like where milk came from.

Serena glanced around the room. "Now *I'm* freaked out."

Mom stood and placed an arm around her shoulder. "There's nothing to be scared of. Spirits were people once, just like us. Sometimes they're just as freaked out as we are, confused too, and they don't know exactly what to do."

"Well, I hope Dad doesn't decide to do that sort of stuff," Serena said. "As much as I'd love him to be around." She rubbed at the inner corner of her eye with her finger.

I slumped on the bed, exhausted. "It's not fair. Why can't Dad just come right out and say what happened to him?"

Mom sat next to me and the bed wobbled. "I want to know the truth too, sweetheart, however painful it might be; but sometimes it's hard for them. They hold back information because it's too painful to relive, or because they're trying to protect us."

"But why do we keep getting visions to do with Riley and his dad when he couldn't even care less!"

"I agree. I'm *over* finding out what he had for dinner and when he put out the garbage." Sasha sat on the bed and sighed.

As if her sitting down propelled me off, I stood, exhaustion dissolving and resolve taking its place. "I'm not putting up with this anymore." I launched myself at the door.

"Savvy, what are you doing?" Mom asked.

My hand poised on the doorknob, I turned back to my family. "I'm going to see Riley, and I'm gonna make him listen."

CHAPTER 16

I stormed across the dark street and stomped up the steps to Riley's porch. My fist pounded the door, and I shifted impatiently while waiting. Huffing, I pounded on the door again until footsteps sounded, and the door opened into the house. Riley stood with arms crossed, creases between his eyebrows, and irritation in his eyes. "What do you want?"

My father back. Your understanding. You.

"I'd give anything to know what happened to my father; and as for yours, I know the truth but you won't even listen!"

He shook his head and rolled his eyes, moving the door in front of him, closing the gap between us. I held up a firm hand and stopped the door from closing. "I'm not leaving until you listen to me. Just give me a few minutes; let me say my piece, and then I'll get out of your life for good if that's what you want."

"Yeah, that's what I want," he said. "I've got no room for liars or deluded people in my life."

His words stung, but I didn't care at that point. All I

cared about was that Robert Pearce's message would be relayed. "I'm not a liar." I pushed open the door and stepped past him into the living room.

"Well, hurry up. The clock's ticking. Say what you need to say." He crossed one foot over the other and leaned against the wall.

The image of the car accident flashed in my mind, then of my dad's ghost, and my nostrils flared as I held back tears. "Your dad didn't commit suicide, Riley." I forced my voice to be steady. "He had a stroke at the wheel. He tried to steer around the bend but lost control of one side of his body. There was nothing he could do. Nothing anyone could have done. It was an accident. A cruel, terrible accident."

Riley's expression remained unchanged. "You done?"

"Riley, I saw your dad. Just like I'm seeing you now, only he had no shadow. It was his spirit. Later on I saw his death; everything *he* saw before he died. I know what he went through." I stepped closer to Riley and stared unblinking into his eyes. "Your father didn't want to die."

His gaze diverted from mine, and I knew my words had reached him in some way. I knew there was an element of doubt in his mind, but I also knew he wasn't quite ready to accept the possibility that his suicide theory had been wrong. He didn't want to be wrong, and he didn't want to stop fighting against something. He needed someone to blame. I didn't know how I knew this, I just knew it by looking in his eyes; it was as though they had transmitted something more than words could say.

"I know it sounds crazy, and I don't blame you for not believing me, but I'm asking you—no—I'm *begging* you to believe me." I grabbed his wrists, and his tendons tightened like thick cords under my grasp. "Everyone has different abilities. You're good with sport, your brother is good with food, and I'm...well, I can see things." I shrugged, and he wrenched his hands away from mine.

"If you really are psychic, and if that's even possible, then why can't you find out what happened to your own dad, huh?" He crossed his arms again. "Why not solve your own family mystery and keep your nose out of mine?"

I dropped my head and a tear dripped down my cheek and onto the floor, disappearing into the carpet. *No. Stop. Please, stop.* I sucked in a breath, hoping to draw some strength along with it, but when I opened my mouth to speak, my voice quivered. "I've seen my dad too. Today."

Riley's eyes widened. "You found him?"

"No. I *saw* him, just as I saw your dad. He died, Riley. My dad died. But I haven't found out how or why." I dabbed at the corner of my eyes with my fingers and glanced up at the ceiling.

Riley's hand brushed against my arm, and then he lifted it and ran it through his hair, as though he couldn't decide whether to comfort me or call for psychiatric help.

Keep it together, Savannah. You can grieve later. This is about him and his father.

"Anyway, I'm not here to talk about that. I'm here to do what your dad asked me to do. To tell you his death was an accident. And I've done that. I don't know what else to say to make you believe me, but..."

I froze. *Hang on, yes I do.* I dashed down the hall and into Riley's room.

"Hey! What do you think you're doing?" He followed.

I pointed to the volleyball resting on the shelf. "This

rolled off that day after our argument. It rolled off and across the hallway into the bathroom."

Riley's mouth opened slightly, and he scratched behind his ear. "What are you talking about? What's the ball got to do with anything?"

I walked into the bathroom, following the route the ball had taken. I bent and held out my hands to the floor. "You picked it up from here." I walked back into the room. "And put it back on the shelf."

Riley's mouth moved but no words came out; his gaze moved back and forth between the bathroom and the bedroom.

"I know it happened because I saw it."

This clearly made him uncomfortable; he crossed and uncrossed his arms. "Have you been stalking me or something? Peeking in through the window?" He frowned.

I stood in the middle of the hallway and gestured toward the living room, and then toward the frosted glass of the bathroom window. "How could I, Riley?" No one standing outside would be able to see this part of the house.

I walked into the kitchen and sat at the table, and Riley, along with his confused expression, followed. "You like pasta, huh?" I asked, a sense of empowerment washing over me at the accuracy of my ability. "You ate it on Sunday night, right here." I jabbed my finger on the table in front of me. "And for no apparent reason, you shivered. The room went cold."

As if remembering, Riley brought his hands to his arms and rubbed them awkwardly; his eyes moved left and right as though paranoid someone was watching.

I stood. The chair screeched behind me. I edged over

to Riley, standing close to the wall as if for support. "It was him," I whispered. "It was your dad trying to get through to you."

He shook his head. "No, no, no. I don't believe it."

"I know you felt it. I know you wondered if it was him. It's okay."

He turned in a confused circle, his arms moving loosely around as if they didn't know what to do; as if they craved something to hold on to in order to keep steady. "That stuff isn't possible. It can't be. When you die, you die. That's it."

"But how do you know?" My eyes searched his and he looked away. "You don't know. But *I* do." I pressed my fingers to my chest in two sharp movements.

His eyes eased their way around to face me, cautious, yet curious, desperate even. Desperate to understand the truth. "You're right about the ball, and the pasta, and the cold, but that doesn't prove my dad was somehow...here."

My few minutes were long gone, and he hadn't kicked me out yet. I had to persist. "What about the photo and the lights?"

"The what?" His eyebrows rose.

"You were looking at your dad's photo; one that you'd packed away in a cardboard box. You were upset, and then the lights flickered," I recalled. "I'm guessing it kinda freaked you out a tad."

"How could you even know that? I was in his room; the windows were covered, so unless you planted some sort of spy cam in here, I don't understand how—"

I grabbed his hands. "I didn't need a spy cam. I saw it, in here." I released a hand and pointed to my head. His hand trembled beneath mine, and he pulled it away gently and flexed his fingers as if to steady them.

"What was he wearing on the day he died? Can you tell me that?" Riley asked, his chin raised, testing me with his eyes and trying to regain control of the situation. Something told me he didn't like anyone else to have the upper hand.

I closed my eyes and summoned the memory in my mind. I'd been in Robert's point of view so I couldn't see much. A brown sleeve? Jeans? I couldn't be sure.

"Open your eyes," a voice whispered from somewhere. I inched them open. Beyond Riley's shoulder, standing in the hallway, was Robert Pearce.

I resisted a gasp, not wanting to freak Riley out; and Robert held a finger to his lips as if to shush me. He ran his hands down over his body in a kind of flourish and gave an awkward smile. "Riley never thought much of my fashion sense," he whispered. Then he pointed to an emblem attached to his jacket—brown, by the way. I was right, and the image grew larger. An eagle.

I drew a deep breath and looked Riley in the eye. "He wore jeans, a flannelette shirt, and a brown corduroy jacket."

Riley eyed me curiously. "Anything else?"

"The jacket, it had an emblem of an eagle on it." I pressed my lips together in satisfaction. "Oh, and your dad said you never thought much of his fashion sense."

"Holy crap." Riley released a loud laugh, which surprised me. "And you just…saw all this…in your head?" He squinted.

I nodded.

"Can you see *everything* that goes on here?"

"Don't worry. Your singing in the shower habit is safe with me." I winked, and his face softened.

Robert mouthed, "Give it time," then faded away, which

was good, because it was one thing to tell Riley I'd seen his father and a whole other thing to tell him his father was here, *right now.*

Riley's eyes seemed to search inside his mind. "But my dad, he was depressed. He said life wasn't worth living without Mom."

"I'm not saying that's not true, but on that awful day, death was definitely not on his mind. He was on his way home—to you."

"But if this is all true, it changes everything. I...I still don't know...I'm not sure..."

I grasped his arms. "All you have to do is believe it. Accept it. Take your time to process everything."

Riley exhaled heavily, as though he'd been holding his breath the whole night. "I need some time alone to think about all this. I still can't get my head around the whole... *psychic* thing, let alone what happened to my dad if what you say is true."

"It is true." I turned toward the front door, suddenly tired from all the tension of the night. I stopped at the door and turned my head to face him. I'd reached him. I'd lifted the veil on his ignorance, but now he was exposed. Vulnerable. I'd opened him up to a world he might not be ready for; a world *I* was barely ready for.

As though waiting for the perfect time to arrive home from work, Riley's brother, Leo, pulled into the driveway, and the low hum of the engine died.

"I'll go now," I said. "Good night."

Riley nodded without saying a word, and I closed the door gently behind me. I'd done everything possible to make Riley believe and to do justice to his dad's memory. I needed to leave him alone to deal with the truth, and I hoped like hell that another door would open and lead me to the truth of my own father's death.

CHAPTER 17

It was unusual for me to be the first one up the next morning, but sleep kept escaping me. I rubbed my eyes and went straight to the kitchen, my stomach grumbling. I reached for a banana in the fruit bowl but picked up the piece of paper lodged between the bananas and the apples. A note from Mom:

Morning girls, I've gone for a walk and have something planned for us all. You can have the day off school. Mom xx

Huh. Cool. I put the note back in the bowl and peeled a banana, tore off a brown bit and chucked it into the trash, then devoured the rest in about twenty-five seconds. I went to the front of the house and peered out the window, squinting at the morning light flooding the house. Riley's house looked cold, dark, empty. Thick drapes were drawn behind the windows, and Leo's car wasn't there. Did that guy ever sleep? A car's engine revving turned my head to the right, and Mr. Jenkins eased out of his garage and onto the road, disappearing around the corner. There would be a couple of empty seats in his science class that day. I breathed deeply, relieved I didn't have to handle a day of schoolwork and social navigation.

"Savvy, are you okay?" Serena asked as she emerged from the hallway wearing jeans and a blue and white striped top with three-quarter sleeves. We were nearing the end of summer and a slight freshness sharpened the morning air, but still our sunny weather continued. We probably wouldn't need jackets until the middle of winter.

"I'm fine, why?"

"You're...awake."

I snorted. "I know. Weird, huh?" I gestured to her school bag. "You won't need that. Mom's letting us have the day off. She left a note saying she has something planned for us." I grabbed the note from the kitchen and showed her.

Serena sighed. "Oh. So much for being organized and on time." She retreated to the bedroom to put her bag away, which woke Sasha up. She traipsed into the living room, her wild hair disheveled and mascara smudges under her eyes.

"Someone forgot to wash their makeup off last night," I said.

She flicked a hand at me. "Wasn't exactly a priority."

No, it wasn't. The news about Dad must have really gotten to her; she was normally fanatical about keeping up her strict nightly skin care routine of cleansing, exfoliating, toning, hydrating, moisturizing, and priming, or whatever else she did. Me, if it couldn't be done while in the shower, I didn't bother. There were better ways to spend my time. I grabbed a banana from the fruit bowl and handed it to her; a kind of hope-you're-okay gesture.

"Thanks," she slurred, sleep still evident in her voice.

I showed her the note too, which woke her up. "Awesome. Three-day weekend." She smiled.

Serena reemerged from the bedroom. "Do you think Mom will be okay to perform in the play next weekend?" she asked. "With everything that's happened."

"I think so," I replied.

"Mom wouldn't give up on something she's worked hard for. She'll see it through," Sasha mumbled while chewing her banana.

"Speak of the devil." I turned my gaze to the front door as footsteps click-clacked on the front porch and Mom came in, arms burdened with shopping bags and a bunch of flowers.

"I guess you got my note?" she asked, as Talia and Tamara entered the room all sleepy eyed.

"What note?" Talia asked.

Mom walked into the kitchen and offloaded the bags, and then held up the flowers. "No school today. We're going to do something special. For Dad." She lifted the flowers to her nose and closed her eyes as she breathed in their scent. "Six white lilies, one for each of us. Since we don't have a...*grave* for your father, I thought we could walk over to the cemetery up on the headland and find a spot for him. Somewhere we can go when we want to remember him. And we can each drop a lily into the ocean below, you know, to say good-bye."

As if Mom's psychic abilities had returned, she said, "I know you might not be ready to say good-bye, but I think it's important we do something to acknowledge the fact that he's gone. Something to at least give us a small sense of closure."

"I think it's a great idea," said Sasha, lifting a lily from

Mom's grasp and bringing it to her nose. "And the day off from school, well, that's a bonus too." She winked and Mom smiled.

"Me too," said Tamara. "Maybe we can go out to lunch afterward?"

"Sure," Mom said.

"At Harborside?" I asked Tamara with a cheeky grin. She still hadn't properly met Leo the chef. Maybe I should have taken her with us to the rock-climbing center, although she'd prefer sitting on some rocks in nature and having a picnic than climbing them. I didn't know if Leo worked the lunch shift as well as nights, though he probably did as many shifts as possible to make ends meet for him and Riley. It couldn't be easy for them, and I doubted Riley's video store wages paid much of the bills.

"In the meantime, I need breakfast," Tamara said. "Why don't I whip up some scrambled eggs for all of us, yeah?"

"Knock yourself out," I said.

By nine thirty we were all dressed and ready to walk to the cemetery. After slipping my onyx earrings on, I grabbed my sunglasses and joined the others outside.

We walked via the entrance to the beach, even though it was the long way around. There was no rush; we had time to take the scenic route. The sun warmed my skin as we stepped onto the pathway that led up to the headland. The waves rolled gently onto the shore where children played and parents supervised. An elaborate-looking sandcastle was under construction by a child and his mother, and a vague memory of making one with my dad surfaced in my mind. That's all I had: snippets of memories, flashes of emotion. The rest was lost in the haze of childhood. I'd been only seven when he disappeared and didn't really understand why he couldn't just come home and say, "Girls, look what treats I brought home from the store!" like he used to. Now I understood all too well.

"Looks like we're not the only ones taking the day off," Sasha said, pointing to the beach below us.

Riley strolled along the shoreline, his feet ankle deep in the water, sploshing around as he walked.

"I wonder how he's feeling after last night," I thought out loud.

"Probably just absorbing it all," Mom said. "Give it time."

I chuckled. "That's what his father said."

Mom gave me a knowing smile. "Parents often know what's best."

I wanted to be with Riley the way we were before—before all this—but that was impossible. Whether we would be able to continue where we left off was unknown. Time would tell if we were supposed to be together or if the whole thing was too weird and uncomfortable for him, knowing what I could do.

The pathway curved around until the sandy beach was no longer in view, only the dazzling purplish-blue water of the ocean below. A fresh breeze whipped my hair around my face and lapped at the cotton of my loose T-shirt. Sasha's skirt billowed in the breeze, and Mom pulled her sleeves farther down her arms.

My eyes tingled as we neared the cemetery, as if sensing all the souls that had left this earth. Rows of gray headstones lined up, facing the cliff that overlooked the ocean. Funny. The best views in Iris Harbor were had by those who couldn't really see them. Not the way we could anyway. I knew now they *could* see them, could see any view, anywhere, no matter where they were buried. A woman arranged a small bunch of flowers in the grate on top of a grave, trying to get the perfect balance. Who was she grieving? Her husband? Child? Mother? Or was she grieving her father like we were? Part of me was jealous that she had somewhere concrete to lay her loved one to rest, secure in the knowledge that he or she was at peace. My dad was still out there somewhere, his body anyway, and I didn't know if we would ever find him, but I wouldn't give up. For now, though, it was time to say good-bye to his physical presence, to the hope—the anticipation—that one day he might walk through the door.

Mom stopped at a wooden bench seat that had panoramic views of the ocean, the horizon fading and blending into the sky beyond. "I think this is it. This is his spot."

Talia sat and caressed the wooden slats. "Yes. It's perfect. It feels right."

Mom withdrew keys from her pocket and scratched at the wood on the back of the seat.

"Mom, what are you doing?" Serena asked.

Sasha snorted. "I think our darling mother is vandalizing public property."

"Oh, I am not, I'm just etching your father's initials into the seat. I'm sure the Iris Harbor council won't mind." She shot us a silly look, and I smiled. Confessing our gift seemed to have brought us closer together. Knowing Mom understood and accepted us, could maybe even help us navigate through this new terrain, was a relief.

"There," she said, stepping back and revealing "D.D." permanently engraved into our father's makeshift resting place.

I glanced around, half expecting Dad to appear and show his approval, but the only people visible were my mom and sisters, and the woman in the cemetery whose hands were now joined in prayer.

The seat was only a yard or so from the cliff's edge. It wasn't a straight drop, more of a steep rocky incline, eventually meeting the water whose colliding waves flung themselves upward and slapped against the hard rocks leaving behind a slippery black gloss. My sisters joined Talia on the seat. There wasn't enough room for all of us at once, so Mom and I stood behind it with our hands resting against the back support. Mom's hands rubbed against the fresh inscription, a link to her husband.

"Dad would have loved this view," Mom said. "I hope he can see it." She glanced at me as if to ascertain whether I could see him nearby.

"I'm sure he can," I replied, and I knew she knew that meant "no."

Serena sniffled, and Talia placed a comforting arm around her younger sister.

"What do you remember about him, girls?" Mom asked. "I know you were young, but…"

"We used to play with Legos together," Serena whispered. "For hours. He'd build these enormous houses and get me to help. He was so patient."

"I remember that too," added Sasha. "Though I didn't have as much patience as you two. I preferred playing with my Barbie dolls!"

"That'd be right." Serena turned her head to Sasha and smiled.

"He and I used to make double-decker sandwiches," Tamara said as she held up her hands to indicate size, "this big. We'd put anything and everything on them, and he'd never question what I chose to add. No matter if I put peanut butter with ham and chili sauce, he still took a bite and said it was delicious."

"Oh yeah, I think you gave me a bite of that one, Tamara," said Talia. "You said it was a super sandwich and I'd get superpowers. I swore I could jump farther off my bed with that towel hanging from the back of my neck like a cape." She laughed.

"Well, it must have worked, look at us now." Tamara glanced around at us all. She was right. We had developed our own kind of superpower.

"What else do you remember, Talia?" Mom asked.

"His hugs." She squeezed Serena tighter. "Sometimes I can still feel his arms around me, if I close my eyes and concentrate really hard."

"His smile," I said. "His wide, happy smile. He had this way of making you feel like everything was all right. Like his smile was some kind of sensing device; when you saw it you just felt...safe. Secure."

"Oh, I do miss that smile." Mom put her arm over my shoulder. The white lily hung from her slender fingers next to my neck; its large petals lifted gently in the breeze. "Your smile is very similar to his, Savvy." She looked at me and I couldn't help but flash a grin, as though I was channeling Dad and it was actually *his* smile coming to life through mine.

I looked back to the ocean, the rippling surface sending ripples of emotion through my heart, my body, my soul. Even though Dad was gone, he would always be here, in a way. Just like the ocean: ever present, gracing the world with its gentle presence. Even if you couldn't see it, you knew it was there, somewhere.

Mom dropped her arm from my shoulder and walked to the edge of the cliff; and like birds flying south, we followed our leader. "David. No matter what happens from now, I will always love you. If you were here, alive, right now, and walked up to me, I would drop everything and be with you. I wouldn't let you out of my sight. But I know you've moved on somewhere new, and I know you might not fully comprehend what's happened, but you reached out to Savannah, our daughter. You had the strength to show her the truth. That's a sign that your soul is evolving, coming to terms with whatever happened. When the time is right for you to show us more, we'll be ready. We'll be here. You can count on us."

Mom's voice quivered and she wiped at her eyes. "Thank you for being a part of my life, for giving me five beautiful daughters, and for being you. I'll never forget you." She held the lily up to the sky, and then released it with a calm but definite toss over the cliff, watching as it floated to the rocky, watery depths below. She kissed the palm of her hand and held it out.

One by one my sisters said their good-byes too and tossed their lilies into the ocean. When it came to my turn and I said good-bye, I knew it wasn't really good-bye. I knew I'd see him again, sometime. I knew he'd find a way to lead us to what happened, to the truth. And I'd be patient. As both Robert Pearce and Mom had said, "Give it time." Maybe they weren't only referring to Riley.

See you soon, Dad.

I held the lily to my nose and breathed in its fresh, sweet scent and with the image of Dad's smile held firmly in my mind, I threw the flower far out into the ocean as though it were a volleyball and I was aiming for the win. It went farther than any of the others. I knew we weren't in competition, but it was my way of showing Dad how much I loved him. How much I was prepared to do what was necessary to find out the truth, lay him properly to rest, and live the full life that he gave me.

• • •

After a surprisingly happy day with my family, we ordered Chinese food, Dad's favorite, and sat in the living room in our pajamas playing Monopoly. Serena won, thanks to her cautious and strategic nature, whereas Sasha had long been bankrupt and spent a few too many times in jail. Mom had tried to share some cash with her, but Serena wouldn't let her. "You have to play by the rules, Mom," she'd said.

At just after ten, we packed up the game and Mom put on some music, some sort of new agey relaxing stuff that was strangely comforting. A year ago I would have scoffed at it and put on the top-forty countdown instead, but things had changed. I'd changed.

I sipped the last of my hot chocolate when a knock at the door sounded. It was a bit late for visitors. Mom tied up her dressing gown and went to the door, peering first through the window nearby, then unlocking and opening the door. "Riley, hello. How can I help you?" Mom asked, and my eyelids jumped open. He'd never come to the front door before.

"Hi, Mrs. Delcarta, sorry it's late. I've just finished my shift at the video store and was hoping to speak to Volley—*Savannah*," he said, and a smile tickled my lips.

"Sure, come on in," Mom said.

"Oh no, it's okay, I don't want to disturb you all. I'll just wait here," I heard him say.

I took Mom's place at the door as she ushered my sisters into the kitchen. "Hi," I said.

"Hi." He eyed my outfit, and I resisted a gasp upon looking at my feet; they were covered by fluffy black Cheshire cat slippers. "They suit you," he said with a hint of a smile.

At least I was wearing my plain stripy pajama shorts and white T-shirt instead of my matching Cheshire cat nightie with the sparkling, glittery eyes.

"I wanted to say I'm sorry," he said. "Sorry for being such an ass and calling you a freak."

I stepped outside onto the porch and closed the front door behind me. "It's okay; it was understandable. It's not every day someone tells you what I told you."

"No, but I should have listened to you instead of demanding you get out of my house. I feel really bad. If I could take it back I would."

"Hey," I said. "We can't change the past, remember?"

"Unfortunately, no."

"But we can decide how the future might unfold, at least to a certain degree."

The moon shone high behind him, casting a glow around his body like an aura. Or was it an aura? It had a tinge of blue in it.

"Do you forgive me?" he asked. His eyes were soft and vulnerable. "It's okay if you don't, but—"

"I forgive you."

His shoulders relaxed. "I just wanted you to know how bad I felt. Especially now that I know you're telling the truth."

"So you believe me? Those things I told you last night, about your father being with you, you believe it was him?"

"I *know* it was."

Wow. A rewarding sense of warmth flooded inside me; and for the first time since I'd developed this gift, I felt like it was making a difference.

"Just like I know the sudden downpour we had earlier today was him. His way of showing me that he was listening, that he was there."

"What?" It had poured with rain after we tossed our lilies into the ocean and started walking back down the pathway of the headland. Right out of nowhere, clouds had appeared and released their load.

"Yeah, it was amazing. I was sitting on the beach and I asked him for a sign. I know he gave me three back home, but I needed something else, something more. Some way to know he could hear me. I even gave him ideas, like making the breeze go really cold or having one of the children playing in the sand call out my name, or finding a shell in a certain spot. Then I suggested that maybe he could even make it rain, and I was kind of joking because I didn't really believe that was possible. After a while I gave up and thought maybe he wasn't really around, that those things back home were just my imagination playing tricks and that somehow you were playing along, so I got up to head back home. Then it started. Big drops of heavy rain poured down on me, and I couldn't believe it. I laughed like I hadn't laughed in ages;

and while others scurried to get under cover, I stood there and welcomed it."

Double wow. My smile widened. "So I've got *you* to thank for the drenching I got today, huh?"

"You weren't at school?"

"Nope. We all had a day off. I hope you know Sasha was very annoyed that her hair went frizzy after the rain."

He laughed. "Happy to be of service." Then he shook his head side to side. "I can't believe this is happening, I mean, it's *so* way out. But I do believe it. Somehow, this is real." He grasped my hands in his. "I believe it. And I believe *you*."

His touch and his words sent bubbles of happiness going off in my belly. "I'm glad."

"So what you said about my dad's death, you really saw it? You know what happened?"

I nodded. "I did. As I said before, I believe he had a stroke and it was definitely no suicide."

Riley blinked his eyes tightly and clamped his lips together with a nod. "Thank you," he said, his eyes glistening in the moonlight and the soft warm glow of our porch light.

"Tell him I would never have left him. I would never have abandoned my children." My gaze darted to the source of the voice behind Riley. Robert Pearce stood on my front lawn.

"What? What is it?" Riley asked, as I stood there, hypnotized by the sight of someone from the other side. Would I ever get used to this?

I gulped and looked Riley in the eye. "Your dad, he's here."

Riley spun around. "Where? He's here, as in right

now? You can see him?" The words blurted from his mouth. "Dad?"

"He's just there." I pointed, and Riley turned to face what was invisible to him. "He wants me to tell you that he would never have willingly left you on your own."

"I know that now. It's okay," Riley said. "Can you tell him I'm sorry?"

"You can tell him yourself."

Riley took a deep breath and ran his hand through his hair. "I'm so sorry, Dad, for thinking the worst. It just seemed the most logical reason for what happened. Everyone agreed and I went along with it."

"I don't blame you, son. You were in pain; you needed someone to blame."

"He says he doesn't blame you. You were just reacting to the pain."

"I wish I hadn't wasted so much time being angry." Riley lowered his head. "I should have given you the benefit of the doubt." He rubbed his temples and raised his gaze toward me. "Did anything cause the stroke? Was it stress?"

I raised my eyebrows at Robert, who could hear what Riley was saying.

"Tell him there was nothing I could have done. I'd had really high blood pressure for a while; even the meds weren't keeping it in check. If it didn't happen on the road, it might have happened at home. And I'm so glad he and Leo weren't in the car at the time."

"He had uncontrolled high blood pressure and thinks it was only a matter of time. He's glad it was only him in the car," I recalled his words as best as I could for Riley.

Riley nodded his understanding.

"Also tell him that in that car I was listening to the playlist he'd made for his mother when she was sick. If it's any consolation, the music provided some comfort for me in those final moments, as it did for her."

I told Riley, and his eyes widened.

"Do you remember her favorite song on the playlist, Dad?"

I listened to Robert's answer then repeated it to Riley, "Let it Be."

His face softened with emotion, and he shook his head in amazement.

"You need to live the life that I couldn't, Riley. Don't waste it being angry or sad, make the most of it. There are so many good years ahead of you." He spoke directly to Riley and approached him, his hand outstretched. He rested it against his son's shoulder, which twinged a little. The sight gave me goose bumps.

"He says you need to make the most of your life, don't be angry or sad anymore. There is so much more for you to experience."

"I will, Dad, I will. I won't let you down."

"You could never let me down." He placed his other hand on Riley's other shoulder, and Riley's hand made its way on top of it, as though he sensed his touch.

"Riley, your dad's hands are on your shoulders."

Riley's eyes widened. "I can feel them. *Just*...like a feather."

"He says you could never let him down."

Riley smiled. "Is Mom there with you?"

I listened to Robert and translated for Riley. "He says he's seen her but hasn't crossed over yet to where she is. He wanted to make sure you'd be okay first."

"I'll be okay, Dad. I am okay. Go to her. Say hi from me; tell her I miss her, please?"

"He will," I said.

"Keep an eye on him, will you?" Robert said to me. "Don't let him forget what I've said."

"I won't."

"What's he saying?" Riley questioned.

I flicked my hand. "Oh, he just wants you to keep up the good singing in the shower." Riley's eyes widened. "I'm kidding! He told me to make sure you remember this, remember what he said."

"How could I forget it?" Riley held up his hand gently, and Robert touched it, though it looked more like it was merging with it. Then Robert took a few steps back.

"The other Savannah is waiting for me," Robert said to me with a wink.

I smiled. "I wish I could have met her."

He waved at me then looked at his son and did some kind of hand movement, like sign language. His hand curved over in an arc, and then his thumb pointed backward as though he was pointing to something behind him.

"What's that?" I asked.

"Show Riley, he'll tell you," he replied.

With curiosity creasing my brow, I lifted my hand. "Riley, your dad said to show you this." I copied the hand movement he'd done.

Riley crumpled to his knees and a tear fell from his eye. "Over and out." He repeated the movement himself and said it again, "Over and out."

I glanced at Robert who'd moved farther backward and

had tears of joy in his eyes. His smile was wider than the stretch of ocean on the horizon. Riley sat on the grass, and I joined him, putting my arm around him.

"Dad used to do that hand signal when I was a kid. I can't remember how old I was…"

"You were four," Robert said.

"Four years old?" I asked.

"Yeah, about that. Anyway, I'd had a string of bad ear infections and it affected my hearing for a while. My parents were worried my speech might not progress as it should, and they taught me some sign language. Even after my hearing returned, we continued using some of the signs. This particular one, Dad had made up himself." Riley did it again. "He'd do it after putting me to bed, instead of saying good-night, he'd say "Over and out." It became our thing."

"That's so sweet." I glanced up at Robert and smiled, his body fading slightly. "I think he's doing it now, not to say good-night, but to say…" I couldn't get the word out.

"Good-bye," Riley said, his eyes looking distant. His Adam's apple bobbed as he swallowed, and then he spoke again. "It's okay, Dad. I understand. It's time to go."

"I love you, Son. And when Leo is ready for the truth, tell him I love him too." Robert turned away, and I repeated his words to Riley.

"I love you too, Dad." Robert turned halfway around at his son's words, and Riley's gaze looked right at where his father stood, as though he could see him too. Robert did a final over and out, and Riley's hands did the same. Their final one. Their last good-bye. And it brought a tear to my eye.

"Thank you," Riley said to me, and I gave him a you're-welcome smile. When I turned my gaze back to Robert, he was gone.

"Is he…" Riley asked.

I nodded. "He's gone."

Riley's chest expanded as he sucked in a sharp, deep breath and released it loosely as his head dropped into his hands. I took his hands in mine; the moisture from his tears ran across my palm. We sat like that together until his breathing returned to a normal rhythm, and he turned his head toward mine.

"What about *your* dad?" he asked.

"It's okay. We don't have to talk about that. Tonight's about you and your dad."

"No, I want to know. When you mentioned that you saw him, I still didn't believe; and there you were suffering and I didn't even help you."

"It's okay. A lot happened that day."

"So, you've seen him, just like my dad?"

"Yep. Just once."

"Did he tell you what happened to him?"

"Nope. But I'm sure one day we'll find out." There was no need to burden him with how Dad had warned us about someone.

"I'm sorry. I mean, I guess it's good in a way that you know for certain he's gone, but that doesn't make it any easier."

"There is a sense of relief, and at least there's a bit of closure—but yeah, it's hard." I hung my head. "But we gave him a nice send-off today on the headland at the edge of the cemetery. We made a 'spot' for him on one of the bench seats."

"That's good. Now you'll have somewhere to go when

you want to feel close to him."

"Yeah."

Riley's gaze narrowed. "So you *all* gave him a send-off? Your Mom too?"

"Um, yeah. I told her."

"About seeing your dad? And she believed you?"

I smiled. "She did." I resisted telling him about my mother's past experience as a psychic. I wasn't sure if she wanted other people to know, especially now that her abilities had faded. "She knows about all of us."

"That's right. You said it's not just you. That all your sisters have this ability too."

"Yes, can you believe it?" I asked.

"Right now, I'd believe anything." He grinned.

"None of my sisters can see spirits, only me. And when we sense something, I'm the only one who sees things. Serena can hear things, Sasha smells things, Tamara tastes things, and Talia can feel things. Five sisters. Five senses."

"One awesome gift," Riley added.

I smiled. "I'm starting to think you might be right on that." I hugged him closer and he slid his arm around my waist as we sat there on the grass, my legs cold in the night air and my fluffy slippers looking out of place in the outside world. A satisfied buzz vibrated inside. I'd made a difference. This bizarre, unexpected gift we'd been given had actually helped someone. Maybe it wasn't the traumatic thing we'd thought it was. Along with my sisters, I could really help people and give them peace of mind and closure. If that was the case, then it would be worth it. As for that other vision of the fire, it had yet to happen. Maybe it *wouldn't* happen. Maybe by helping Riley we'd somehow affected the future, changed it from what it would have been to what it was meant to be. I could only hope.

Riley nudged me with the side of his body. "So, ah, do you think you can predict my future?" He eyed me both hopefully and cautiously.

I tapped my chin with my finger. "Hmm...let me see." I rolled my eyes upward and pretended to think, then moved my fingers to his face and ran them across his cheekbone. "I do foresee something in your future." I leaned closer. "This."

When my lips were only an inch away from his, he intercepted and put his finger on them. "Wait," he said. "I'm just getting over a bad cold; I don't want you to catch it."

I kissed his finger and said, "I don't care. I've been through heaps worse than a bad cold. I can handle it. And maybe I won't catch it anyway."

"Believe me, the first day was a shocker. I was both hot and cold—with the chills—and I had a major sore throat. And the number of tissues I went through, you don't wanna know, and—"

"Riley." I matched his previous gesture and put my finger on his lips. "Shut up and kiss me."

The corners of his mouth turned upward into a smile, as did mine. He leaned toward me and my smile met his in one sweet, luscious, unforgettable kiss. Our first had been just like heaven, but this was better. It was heaven on earth.

CHAPTER 18

One thinks she can handle a cold, but when she gets said cold, she thinks otherwise. I disposed of my hundredth tissue for the morning and grabbed another. The timing couldn't be worse. Thanks, Riley. Then again, I'd kinda got myself into this mess.

"Oh, you poor thing, sweetheart. Such a shame." Mom placed a cold cloth on my forehead. "You'll have to stay home tonight, I'm afraid."

"No, I can't miss your play! I might be okay by then if I rest all day," I said.

"I doubt it. Besides, you don't want to go infecting everyone. Most of the town will be there tonight. You could start an epidemic."

"Oh, Mom, don't be so dramatic."

"I can't help it. I'm just getting in some practice." She gave a dramatic bow. "Anyway, by the looks of it we'll be doing another play sometime down the track. You can go to that one."

"Unless she gets sick for that one too," said Sasha. "Thanks to you, we'll probably all come down with the bug and our house will become a hospital."

"You can thank Riley. He's the one I caught it from."

"Oh, too much kissy-kissy, huh?"

"Sasha! Leave your sister alone and let her rest. Now help me pack my costumes."

They fumbled with bags and costumes and props while I closed my eyes and hoped the cloth would reduce my fever. I pulled the blanket up to my chin as the rest of my body was cold, and then kicked it off when I got too hot again. This was going to be a totally sucky way to spend a perfectly good Saturday.

• • •

"All right, I think that's everything. Or maybe it's not. What am I forgetting?" Mom spun around aimlessly. "Oh, I haven't done the washing up! I really should get those pans soaking in soapy water before I go, I don't want—"

"Mom, leave it. We better get going. The dishes can wait. They need you there early, remember? And we have to help set up the chairs," Talia said.

"Yes, you're right." The microwave pinged and Mom dashed into the kitchen, returning with a mug of hot soup. "Okay, now, Savvy, get this into you. There's extra in the fridge if you need it. Keep refreshing your cloth in the water bowl, and don't forget to take your third dose of those herbal immune support tablets." She placed them on the coffee table next to me.

"I won't."

"Your phone is right there too. And make sure you call me if there's any problem, okay? I'll check my messages in between every scene to make sure."

"Mom, I'll be fine. Riley said the first day was bad and then it got better. I've just got to ride it out."

"You sure you don't want Talia to stay with you?"

Talia rolled her eyes. Oh the joy of being the eldest sister. Being the youngest had its disadvantages too, though.

"No, there's nothing she can do; she'll just annoy me. I'll lie here and watch movies and go to sleep. No need for more of us to miss your performance."

"Well, if you're sure?"

"I'm sure."

"Right then, c'mon girls. Let's get this show on the road!"

"If you see Riley, tell him thanks a lot," I called out as they filtered out the front door.

"Will do!" Sasha replied, and the door closed behind them.

Ah, peace at last. It was hard to get that in this house. Privacy and time alone were luxuries reserved only for the bathroom, and even then there was often someone banging on the door asking you to hurry up. Usually Sasha.

I pressed play on the DVD and slurped the chicken soup; the comforting heat washed away the pain in my throat. It felt like razor blades in there. I finished it all up then opened the bottle of pills and took two out. They were large, brown, and oval shaped, and they tasted disgusting if you managed to get a bit of it on your tongue before swallowing. I had no clue what was in them, but with Mom's insider knowledge of natural health stuff, I trusted her judgment.

I popped them in my mouth one at a time and followed

each with a swig of water. Ew… gross. A hint of their bitter taste brushed over my tongue. The taste alone should be enough to kill the suckers multiplying inside me.

A slight bubbly sensation fizzed inside. Déjà vu. The pills…there were pills in that vision we'd had ages ago. Could this be important? But I took vitamin tablets every day, and it'd never crossed my mind till now. It was probably nothing.

I drank the rest of the water and lay back on the couch with a freshly cooled cloth. My mind drifted in and out of consciousness, and I couldn't really comprehend what was going on in the movie; my mind was too foggy. Eventually I succumbed to my heavy eyelids and closed my eyes, welcoming the darkness.

When my eyes opened, I squinted at the light and noticed the movie had reverted to the main menu. I'd missed the end. Oh well. It was a weekly rental, and even if it wasn't, I was sure Riley would turn a blind eye if I returned it a day late.

I eased myself up and trudged to the bathroom. On the way back I paused near Mom's room. For some reason I thought I'd seen a small flash of light. Maybe it was just my cold or even the pills, who knows? My body wanted to lie back down, but my mind was drawn to Mom's closet. The box. Her collection of stuff from her psychic days. She'd already shown us, but I was sure she hadn't shown us everything that was in there.

Like a curious cat, I tiptoed into the room and switched on the bedside lamp. *I'll just take a quick look.* I pulled over the stool that sat in front of her dressing table and stepped onto it, keeping my balance by holding onto the closet door. I slid the top of the closet open and pushed aside the blankets, revealing the tattered old shoebox. I pulled it out and brought it to the bed, lifting off the lid and unwrapping the purple fabric. I picked up Mom's business cards for another look, shaking my head at how we never knew Mom's secret and how somehow she'd passed her gift onto us to share between ourselves. There was also a box of tarot cards; she hadn't shown us those. I wondered if they could help enhance our visions and make better sense of them. There was also a half-empty (was I becoming a pessimist?) bottle of aromatherapy spray. Cleansing room spray, it was called. If it hadn't been used for nine years, I guessed it was probably out of date; if aromatherapy oils even went out of date. I resisted spraying it, even though my nose was curious, as I didn't want Mom smelling it when she got home and finding out I'd been snooping. I looked through the rest of the items. Nothing else that interesting. I was about to put the lid back on when I noticed the inner corner of the bottom of the box was curled upward like it was coming unstuck. I picked at it a bit and it lifted up; a flash of white caught my eye. I removed the box's contents and lifted the bottom layer of cardboard, revealing a white envelope underneath with its edges slightly brown.

My darling Rose, was handwritten in blue ink on the front. I picked it up and turned it, my hands tingling with anticipation. The seal had been opened before and was taped back in place. My finger hesitated at the edge of the seal, wanting so much to lift the flap and see what was inside; but after testing the edge ever so slightly, I knew it would rip the paper off the envelope if I opened it. Mom would know I'd looked. If she ever checked. Maybe I should just ask her about it, tell her I wanted to check out her business cards again and the box tipped over and the envelope fell out?

I looked at the handwriting again. It must have been written by my dad, because the paper was too old to have been given to her recently; and I didn't know if Wayne and Mom were at the my-darling stage yet, though I guessed it wouldn't be long. She'd continued seeing him after finding out about Dad's death, though I was sure she hadn't yet told him about her past profession. Maybe she wouldn't. Maybe she wanted to leave the past where it belonged and move forward to a new beginning.

I remembered my silent promise to Dad that I'd never give up on him, and the urge to open the envelope outweighed common sense. I slid my finger under the edge of the seal and lifted it gently...

Knock, knock!

I gasped, dropping the envelope. Someone was at the front door. Maybe Mom had come down with stage fright and couldn't go through with the performance, or maybe she'd had second thoughts about leaving me home alone and sent Talia back to look after me.

I shoved the envelope back under the layer of cardboard and replaced all the items in the box, then returned it to the back of the closet, and put the stool back in front of the dressing table.

I walked to the front door and peered out the side window. Mr. Jenkins stood on the porch. His eyes caught mine, and he offered an awkward smile. I closed the drapes and put my hand on the doorknob. *Wait. Should I open it?* It would look strange if I didn't. He was just my science teacher. But who was he out of school hours?

I tentatively opened the door, but only a fraction,

using the excuse of having a cold and that I didn't want to pass it on.

"I was just on my way to the school play and noticed a light was on inside the house. I thought I'd check if anyone needed a lift to the school hall."

"Oh, no, thanks anyway. Mom left earlier and my sisters went too." Crap. Just revealed that I was home alone. *Good one, Savannah.*

"You sure you don't want to come? I can take you there. It's not the best idea to stay home alone." He'd barely said two words to us the whole time he'd lived there, why the sudden concern?

"Um, no, thanks anyway. I really need to rest and get over this cold. It's a shocker. Fever, chills, sore throat…" I hoped the threat of a contagious illness would get him to go away.

Creases formed in Mr. Jenkins's forehead. "I see. Well, I'll be off then. The play starts in fifteen minutes and I don't want to be late." He turned away, and then turned back again. "Don't forget to lock the door behind you," he said then walked off.

When I locked the door and made sure the drapes were tightly closed, I realized my heart was racing. From illness or fear? Was I making too much of this? Then a memory flashed in my mind. The vision. I'd seen Mr. Jenkins at a door, just after I'd seen the pills. *Oh no.* I raced into the kitchen and checked that the oven was off and checked all the bedrooms to make sure no candles were alight. Was I at risk being here alone? I peered through every window and scanned the surroundings, making sure there wasn't anyone lurking around. Had I heard Mr. Jenkins's car drive off? I couldn't recall it. Maybe he only pretended he was leaving but then went back inside his house, or maybe my mind was playing tricks and I was too sick to think straight.

After several minutes of surveillance had failed to provide any reassurance, I grabbed the laptop and brought it to the coffee table. My legs ached and I needed to sit. Then again, my head ached and I needed to sleep again, but there was no way I could now. I opened up Google and tapped on the side of the keyboard, wondering what on earth I was hoping to find.

I searched for news articles on all the previous fires, hoping to find some sort of clue or link that would help. Maybe it would—pardon the pun—spark something in my mind that could help prevent another fire. I read through them all but nothing jumped out. If only my sisters were here and we could connect. They hadn't had time before they left this afternoon.

I found myself on a website that explained some of the potential reasons that someone would become an arsonist, and I became fascinated by the psychology behind it. I took a sip of water to ease my parched throat, and then before I knew what I was doing, I typed "Mr. Simon Jenkins" into the search engine.

Various links came up regarding teaching and school. On page two I found a link that caught my eye:

"Local Teacher Buries Wife"

I clicked through and read the article about how Mr. Jenkins found his wife dead when he returned home from work one Monday. The autopsy revealed she'd died of a brain hemorrhage, cause unknown. She could have had an undiagnosed aneurysm—the thought of which sent chills up my spine—or she could have fallen and bumped her head badly. But that would have left a bruise on her scalp, surely. The article didn't mention anything else. Or, the alternative that sent even more chills up my spine—foul play. Had she been knocked down, shaken, or hit? All the article was prepared to say was "cause inconclusive."

I took a moment to think about the poor woman and wished she'd pay me a visit and explain how it happened like Riley's dad had done. *Should I get Talia's Ouija board out?* Oh man, this cold was messing with my head. I really should just lie down and rest. But my fingers had other ideas. I refined the search and added "Roach Place" to the links about Mr. Jenkins.

I scrolled down the page until one link in particular sent my heart pounding:

"Roach Place Tragedy"

The article was an archived news report from almost forty years ago. My gaze darted to the part that highlighted the name Jenkins from my search, and my hand flew to my mouth.

Oh my God.

Knock, knock!

My heart practically tripped over itself at the sound of someone knocking on the door, and I instinctively grabbed my phone, my fingers poised and ready to call for help.

CHAPTER 19

I froze. I didn't know whether to look through the window or call my Mom. I crept to the front entrance. Tentatively, I inched the drapes aside a fraction, and on seeing my visitor, I yanked open the door and flung myself at him.

"Riley! I'm so glad you're here." I pulled him inside and locked the door behind us. "Wait, what are you doing here?"

"At intermission I couldn't find you. Sasha said you were home alone suffering with my cold. I felt bad and decided to come over and keep you company. By the looks of it, I made the right choice." He smiled.

"Quick, come over here." I led him to the couch. The laptop was open on the coffee table. "Did you know Mr. Jenkins lived in the same house he does now when he was a child?"

"No, but why is that important?"

"Look." I pointed to the article. "When he was seven years old he saw another kid run screaming out of this house. *Our* house. The boy's mother had died, right here."

I gestured to where we sat, and shivered. "She was an alcoholic and drug addict, who had overdosed. Mr. Jenk— *Simon*—called for his own mother, who ran into the house next door and found the woman dead on the couch. Simon saw the body too." I forced a deep breath. "The boy whose mother died was Wayne. Wayne Rickers. The man who's dating my mother."

"Oh man," Riley said.

"He's been visiting us, having dinner with us, getting close to my Mom, and he never even thought about mentioning that he spent his early childhood in this very house?" I stood, fuming, and then sat as dizziness overtook me.

"You okay?"

I nodded. "What kind of morbid person does that?"

Riley ignored my question as he read the article then clicked on page two, which I hadn't read yet. "Ah, Sav?" he said, eyeing me with concern. He pointed to the end of the article:

After Mrs. Jenkins found the body and called police, she tried to take young Wayne out of the room, but the boy insisted on staying with his dead mother. According to Mrs. Jenkins, Wayne stood by the dying flames in the fireplace, stoking them, and repeatedly mumbling that he needed to keep the fire burning for his mother, that he couldn't let it die out. "Mommy was sick. She told me I had to put three big logs on the fire to keep it burning while I was at school, to make her feel better. I did my best. I made the biggest fire I could. She said I was a good boy for helping her keep warm," the now orphan reportedly said. "If I can make the fire big again, she might wake up. She might not be dead anymore." The traumatized child was eventually removed from the house and placed in foster care.

"Holy crap." I held a shaking hand to my mouth. My

father's words that night, when he'd warned me about someone, reverberated in my ears: "The flames, he needs them. He needs to keep the fire burning. For her. For the one he lost."

Wayne. *Wayne* needed to keep the fire burning. As some deluded way to keep the memory of his mother alive.

Riley grabbed my arm. "Do you think he could be—"

"It has to be him. Oh my God." I told him about my dad's warning and pointed to the exact same words in the newspaper article.

All fatigue and sickness drained from my body. The only heat and chills overtaking me were from the realization that my mother was involved with a messed-up criminal. And even worse...

"Where is he now?" Riley asked.

Fear churned in my belly. "He's with Mom, helping backstage at the play. And the whole town is there!" My hands shook and my breath came in short bursts.

Riley stood and yanked me toward the door. "We have to go, now!"

CHAPTER 20

I grabbed my phone and house keys and my fingers shook as I tried to lock up.

"Here, I'll do it." Riley locked it with a quick twist and handed back the keys. Then we stepped off the porch. "Are you going to be able to do this?"

Heat flushed my face, and I felt strangely out of my body like my mind had moved too fast and left my physical self back in the house, and I was waiting for it to catch up. "I have to. Riley, I had a vision a while back about another fire. People were killed. So far two things out of that vision have already happened tonight. We have to stop it. Let's go!"

Riley turned to his house. "Wait. Can you ride a bike? It would be faster."

"It's been years, but yes. You got a spare?"

He nodded, racing toward his house and pressing the garage remote on his key. "You can take mine. I'll take my brother's."

While waiting for him to retrieve the bikes from the

junk-filled garage, I dialed Mom's number. No answer. I dialed Talia's number, but the ringtone shrilled from inside the house. *Geez, Talia.* There was no response from Sasha's phone either; she probably turned it off for the performance.

Riley wheeled the bike over to me. "We need to call for help first," I said. "We should get the police there." My feet wanted to run or ride, and get there as quickly as possible, but logic told me to take a few more moments to call the authorities and hope like hell they didn't put me on hold. But what would I say? I had a vision and now it's coming true? Google told me that Wayne seemed obsessed by fire after his mother died and therefore he must be the arsonist? It sounded ridiculous when put that way, but when I put everything together, all the details, it made perfect sense. I remembered Wayne's fascination with our fireplace turned bookcase that night he came for dinner for the first time, and I whipped out my phone from my pocket.

"No, you start riding. I'll call while I ride." Riley pressed his phone and held it to his ear, then got onto his bike and started pedaling. "Hi, I need police over at the high school hall. I have reason to believe the arsonist is going to strike again," Riley said as we rode toward town. "What reason? I just came across some information. Look, we need you there ASAP. We believe the arsonist is Wayne Rickers." He was silent for a moment, and I willed my legs to cooperate and push forward. "Another fire? Where? Never mind, please, just get there as soon as you can."

"What did they say?" I asked when Riley shoved his phone in his pocket.

"They're short-staffed. Most of the cops are out at another incident on the edge of town. Another fire on some guy's property. They said they'll get to the school as soon as they can."

I couldn't see Riley's expression as my surroundings blurred alongside me while we sped down the street, but I had the feeling it was creased with worry. There was no guarantee we could stop this, no guarantee the police would arrive in time.

We left the bikes in a heap in front of the school hall and dashed toward the entrance. Riley grabbed my arm. "We don't want to cause a panic. We better walk in discreetly, get your sisters' attention first, and maybe one of the teachers.

Teachers. Mr. Jenkins. Only moments ago I thought he was the arsonist, and now he could be someone who could help us.

I nodded and sucked in air, trying to catch my breath as sweat dripped down my face. We entered the foyer and passed the two teenage attendants deep in conversation in the food stall, who didn't even acknowledge our presence. Riley quietly opened the door, and we slipped inside the dark hall to the sound of emphatic voices on the brightly lit stage commanding the crowd. We inched along the sidewall, peering into the audience until Sasha's sparkly headband caught my eye. She was rubbing her nose. Serena was rubbing her ear, and Talia was fiddling with her hands. Tamara looked like she'd eaten a sour grape. My eyes urged them to look my way. I caught Sasha's first and waved my hand urgently, instructing her to come over. She nudged the others and they shuffled in their seats, and then crept along in a crouched position so as to not obstruct people's view.

"What's going on? Savvy, why are you here?" Talia whispered, placing her hand on my hot head. "You're burning up. C'mon, let's get you a glass of water."

"We'll all be burning up if you don't listen to me." I dragged her out to the foyer and the others followed. "It's Wayne. Wayne's the arsonist. Where is he?"

"What the? He's probably backstage. So is Mom. All of the cast is on stage right now for this scene, except Mom. She'll be getting ready for her grand finale."

"Oh no." I ran a hand through my damp hair, dislodging the strands that had stuck to my face.

"Wait. It's Wayne? How do you know?" Serena asked.

"There's no time to explain. We have to get Mom out of here. We have to stop him."

The door opened and Mr. Jenkins joined us in the foyer. "Is everything all right?"

"Actually, sir, we may need your help." Riley explained the situation without mentioning anything about the vision, and Mr. Jenkins shot into action.

"I'd had my suspicions about him since he arrived back in town after all these years. Maybe I should've told the police." He shook his head. "Right, you two…" he said as he pointed at Sasha and Serena, "wait outside for the police. And you three, come with me to the side entrance to the backstage area. Wait there and give the police the passcode to get in. It's…" He glanced around to make sure no one else was listening, "Nine nine seven six two three. Got it? Nine nine seven six two three." My sisters nodded, but my eyebrows drew together.

"Wait, what about Riley? And what are you going to do?"

"I'll go backstage and see what's going on. Riley, you can come with me. But we have to be quiet."

"No, I want to come in too. She's my mom, I have to

help her."

"Savannah, we don't know what he's capable of. I can't put you in any danger."

"I may be a girl, but I can take care of myself." I planted my hands on my hips. "Now let's stop wasting time and get on with it." I marched outside where two of my sisters waited with fearful expressions, and the rest of us dashed around the outside of the building. Mr. Jenkins punched in the passcode and Talia repeated it out loud to memorize it, and the men entered the building.

"You sure, Savvy?" Riley asked, turning to face me.

"There's no way I'm staying outside. Let's go." I walked with them down the corridor and past a bathroom. We stopped and pricked our ears, on the alert for the slightest sound. Maybe we should have brought Serena in.

"This way," Mr. Jenkins said. "She might be in the far dressing room at the back." He led the way, and I tried to slow my breathing, still labored from my cold, the bike ride, and the fear.

"Shh," Riley whispered. "I think I hear something."

We stood still, ears angled toward the dressing room door.

A weary, muffled voice wafted through the walls. "But why, Wayne? Why?"

Oh no, she knows. She knows she's in trouble. I forced composure so I could be useful; there was no time to be scared. I had to be ready for action and do whatever was necessary to stop him. I imagined my fear was a clump inside, just like the fear about my aneurysm returning, and blew out all the fragments as quietly as I could. This was it. This was what my visions, *our* visions, had been preparing us for.

"Don't you see?" Wayne's muffled voice said. "This is the only way to make sure we'll be together forever. You, me, and my mother."

Oh my God. The man was crazy.

Mom sobbed. "Please, Wayne. If you love me, let me go. Please untie me, please."

I squirmed at her words.

"No!" he yelled. "This is the only way. This is the final one. The final fire. My mom would be so proud. I've kept the fires burning all these years."

"Final Fire Claims Eight Lives"

The newspaper headline of my vision flashed through my mind. No way in hell was I going to let that come true. I reached for the door handle to the dressing room. Riley grabbed my wrist in a flash before I could touch it.

"Savvy!" he whispered, so quietly it was barely audible. "What if it's locked? If he knows you're here he might... he might..."

"He might act in haste," Mr. Jenkins said. "Just sit tight, let me think." He glanced around as though a solution might manifest in thin air.

"And the cops will be here soon," Riley added.

Mom and Wayne continued talking, arguing, and showed no indication they knew we were here.

"Help!" Mom yelled, but the second half of the word was muffled further as though he'd clamped a hand over her mouth.

"Yell out again, and I'll tape your mouth shut and light this match right now before you've listened to my explanation." His voice was tense, mean, and threatening, and my blood boiled at the sound of it. "Anyway, even if someone were to come, they won't get through that door. It's just you and me, baby."

"Get your hands off me," Mom warned with a determination in her voice I hadn't heard before.

"We were meant to be together, you and me. When I heard that a new family had moved into my house, I kept an eye on it. Imagine my surprise when I saw that a beautiful woman with five beautiful daughters had taken residence within its troubled walls. And with no garage, it was so easy to mess with your car so you'd have to come into the only mechanic's garage in town."

"You did that on purpose?"

Realization dawned inside. So he was the hooded figure I'd seen moving away from our house not long after we moved in.

"It was the perfect excuse to meet you and ask you out. And when you told me you were performing in this play, our fate was sealed. I knew this would be the ideal scene for my final act. Schools cause nothing but trouble. No one came to my rescue when kids bullied me because I had a drug addict for a mother."

"Wayne, I'm sorry you had a hard life, but it's not my fault, it's not—"

"Shut up, Rose."

I flinched.

"You moving into *my* house, it was destiny. It was as though my mother had chosen you for me. And in a moment, you'll be able to meet her."

Mom sobbed again.

A moment? I eyed Riley and Mr. Jenkins with urgency.

We had to do something, or the police would arrive and it'd be too late.

Mr. Jenkins moved slowly along the hall, mouthing "shhh" as he went, and then peered around the corner into what looked like a storage area. He motioned for us to join him. At least it was farther away from where Mom and Wayne sounded like they were, and they shouldn't be able to hear us conspiring.

Mr. Jenkins pointed to a door. "This is a two-way closet. Wayne probably doesn't know that. Before we extended the hall, this used to be the door to this dressing room. It was converted into a storage closet, one on each side. If I remember correctly, there should only be a thin sheet of plywood separating us from them. If I can lift that out of the grooves, I'll be able to get through the door on the other side."

Hope swam inside me, and I was so grateful to have Mr. Jenkins around. Having worked at the school all his life, he knew the place inside out.

"Let's get the ball rolling," Wayne's gritty voice traveled through the walls, muffled but just loud enough to make out. I could also hear the sound of liquid splashing on the ground. "All I have to do is light a match and the beautiful, magnificent flames will engulf us. It'll be quick, I promise you. And then we'll be together forever, bound by destiny."

"Your destiny is in a prison cell, dickhead," Riley muttered.

Absolutely. No way was I prepared to lose both my parents. Mom needed us, and I would not stand back and let him take her from me. "Let's do this," I said with my hand on the doorknob.

"Savannah, maybe you should go wait outside. Let Riley and me handle it."

I pressed my lips together. "I said, let's do this."

"Okay." He sighed. "When I open the internal door, you and Riley help Rose. Untie her and get her out. I'll get Wayne."

Riley stared at Mr. Jenkins. "No offense, sir, but I think I should handle him. You help Mrs. Delcarta."

Mr. Jenkins eyed Riley's muscular frame, and then his own slight build, and nodded. "You're right. As long as you're up for it?"

"One hundred percent. I'll be damned if I'm going to let him get away with this." A fierce determination sharpened his face.

"Just be careful. And whatever you do, don't let him light a match."

"One last kiss, Rose. One last kiss," Wayne said, and Mom's sobbing intensified.

I felt sick in the stomach.

Hang in there, Mom. We're coming. In my mind I called for Dad's help, his guidance, to help us get through this. *Don't let him take her, Dad, don't let him.* I hoped the element of surprise at us barging through a door he thought was just a closet would stun Wayne long enough for Riley to tackle him to the ground.

"There shouldn't be much stuff in the closet. Most of the equipment would be on or near the stage, so hopefully there's room to squeeze through." Mr. Jenkins twisted the door handle and pulled back the door. He paused when a slight creak sounded, then eased it open more slowly. Wayne was still going on about destiny and other crap, and I couldn't wait to get my poor mother out from under his hold. Mr. Jenkins stepped into the narrow closet and ran his hands over the plywood partition at the back. He pushed it slightly and it wobbled a little, creating a small gap on both sides for his fingers to slip through and take hold. It was attached via horizontal grooves at the top and bottom, so Mr. Jenkins gripped the side edges and shifted it back and forth, trying to budge it from its position. Riley took one side, while I stood back to give them room. The thin sheet of wood lifted just out of the top groove, enough to tilt it downward and lift it from the bottom groove. As the wood was placed to the side, the sound of Wayne's voice grew louder now that there was less of a barrier separating us.

"Tomorrow's my birthday, Rose. Did you know that?"

"No, I didn't," Mom's shaky voice replied. "Why don't you celebrate and think things through? I can help you," she pleaded.

"I would have been forty-five. I told myself forty-five was it. No more. I've had enough, Rose. It's time to leave where I don't belong and go somewhere I do. Where *we* do."

"But Wayne, I belong here with my girls. They need me."

My heart ached and I fought back tears. There'd be time for them later. "Ready?" I asked.

They nodded. Riley took the front position, as the priority was to get to Wayne first. Mr. Jenkins was next, then me, lucky last.

"Now, you'll have to think and act fast, Riley. Go straight for Wayne. Get him to the floor if you can."

He nodded. "Looks like my martial arts training might come in handy for the first time in my life," he said, and my sense of hope returned. He'd never told me he had those sorts of skills. Hopefully Wayne didn't have them to match.

"Okay, on the count of three," Mr. Jenkins whispered. "One, two…three!"

Riley barged through the door and we followed. I only saw a flash of Wayne until my eyes darted to Mom, tied up on a chair, her eyes red and swollen, and her mouth gaping in shock at our sudden entrance. I rushed to her side. Mr. Jenkins was already working the ties on her arms, and I dropped to the slippery floor to attack the ones around her ankles. I was so focused on my role, I couldn't see how Riley was going; but grunts and shuffles and thumps filled the room, along with Wayne's almost demonic yelling for Riley to get away.

"Hurry, hurry!" Mom exclaimed, as a box of matches landed near my foot. I grabbed it and put it in my pocket.

Mom's arms were freed, and she put her hands desperately on my head as I untied the second rope around her right foot. I flicked the loose restraint away and Mom stood, sobbing and shaking and flinging her arms around me. No sooner had she done that then Mr. Jenkins shoved us through the closet door.

"Go, get out of here and tell the police to hurry!" Before we left I saw him charge at Wayne on the floor, and with Riley's help, twisted his arms behind his back as Riley held the man's face to the ground.

"Oh, Savvy, you're here! How did you…" Her words were interrupted by footsteps down the hall, and two cops came in, weapons at the ready.

"He's in there!" Mom pointed. "He tried to kill me!"

"Both of you, outside now," one of the cops said, and we ran as fast as we could down the corridor and out of the building that had become our worst nightmare.

"Mom!" Talia ran into Mom's arms, and Tamara grasped my shoulders.

"What happened? Are you all right? Where's Wayne and Riley and Mr. Jenkins?" Tamara's eyes were wide and worried.

"They've got him on the ground. I think it's over. I think we stopped him," I panted out the words and collapsed into my sister's arms, adrenaline and illness making me a trembling mess.

Mom fell to the ground, Talia and Tamara and myself wrapped around her. Sasha and Serena ran over, along with the two teenage attendants from the food stall.

"Oh my God, Mom." Serena, in tears, attached herself to all of us, followed by Sasha. I could have sworn I felt my father's arms around us too. I could smell his comforting aftershave, taste the sweet chocolate treats he used to buy, hear his addictive laugh, and see his beaming smile. There we were, all connected as one. Five sisters. One mother. And Dad's memory. A family. Safe, together, where we belonged.

CHAPTER 21

"Congratulations." I walked around the side of the volleyball net and shook Riley's hand. "It took you a while, but you finally beat me."

"As I said before, I'd just been letting you win the whole time. Me and the boys," he said as he gestured to his teammates, "we had an agreement. But now it's time to lift your game, Volleyball Girl. No more Mister Nice Guy for me."

I narrowed my eyes at him. "When were you ever Mister Nice Guy, huh?"

"I've been nothing *but* nice. What about the time I did this?" He bent down and planted a firm kiss on my lips. "Nice?"

"Could be better," I said, turning the corners of my mouth upside down and feigning indifference.

"How about this?" He slid an arm around my back and the other under my legs, lifting me off the ground.

"Hey! Put me down!"

He carried me to the water and dumped me in with a splash, and then dove in after me and pulled my face to his. His slippery, wet lips cushioned mine and I shivered. "It's freezing! It'll be winter in another month, you know."

"C'mon, don't tell me that kiss didn't distract you from the cold? Just a bit?"

"You've won your first match, in what, forever, and now you're on a roll and want to start a kissing competition or something?"

"Hmm, now there's an idea." He picked me up again and carried me to the sand. "Every kiss I initiate you have to score out of ten and vice versa."

I held back a grin. "Fair enough. I give that a…" I tapped my chin. "Six."

"Is that all?" he said. "Why don't *you* show me whatcha got, then?"

I stepped on his bare feet to give myself height, and pressed my lips to his in what I felt had to at least be a seven.

"Hmm, six and a half?"

I whacked him on the arm.

"Okay, seven."

"That's better."

He grabbed my hand and we walked to our bags. Riley retrieved a towel from his and wrapped it around me.

"What, aren't you going to try for a ten?" I asked.

"Not now. When you least expect it." He tossed my bag and I caught it. "But I won't have to try. I *will* get a ten."

"That'll be for me to decide." I winked.

We walked to the end of the beach and Riley's phone beeped. He checked it, and then turned his head to the right then the left. "Um, I was thinking I might go get some flowers to put on my parents' graves. I've got a lot of catching up to do with Dad's. Come with me?"

"Sure. I'll get some for my dad's spot, too."

"Oh yeah, you haven't shown it to me yet."

"Let's go, then." We crossed the road and walked to the florist on the main street.

Gino, the owner, smiled at us as we entered. "If it isn't the town hero," he said to Riley, shaking his hand. The local newspaper had done a write up of the events at the school play that night, and Mr. Jenkins remarked how grateful he was that Riley had been able to get Wayne away from Rose and stop him from setting the room alight.

"I just did what anyone would have done. And anyway, if it wasn't for Savannah's detective skills, I wouldn't have been there to help in the first place." He winked at me.

The article hadn't mentioned how I came to the conclusion that Wayne was the arsonist, and I didn't want them to know the full details. My little secret would stay between my family and Riley only.

"Then you deserve a handshake too," Gino said, grasping my hand. "On second thoughts, this is more like it." He gathered me in an enthusiastic embrace, his hand patting my back.

"Well, thank you," I said, grinning.

"What can I help you with?" he asked. "Flowers for the lovely lady?" Gino eyed Riley with a suggestive smile.

"Actually, for my parents' graves," Riley replied, looking around the bright explosion of colors on display.

Gino picked up a couple of bunches. "These would be perfect. Long lasting too. For you, on the house."

"Oh, that's okay, I don't expect—"

"No, no, I want to." He handed Riley the flowers, and I recognized white lilies in among them, just like the ones we'd tossed into the ocean.

"Thanks, man." Riley tucked one of the bunches under his arm and shook Gino's hand again.

Gino bent down and picked up a small posy of gerberas wrapped in paper and tied with string. "And these are for you." He handed them to me. "Since I'm sure the young man was planning on getting some for you, too." He winked suggestively at Riley, who smiled and nodded like he'd come up with the idea himself.

"You're very kind, thank you." My cheeks became hot, and the man hugged me again before we stepped back onto the sidewalk of the main street.

"Wow, what a nice man. No wonder Mom likes going there regularly."

"He's a nice *married* man, too, just so you know," Riley said.

"Oh, don't worry. I think my mom has sworn off men for good! Although she's quite fond of her rescuer now. Mr. Jenkins. Did I tell you she invited him over for afternoon tea a couple of weeks after that night, as a thank you?"

"No. That's good. Maybe he's slowly coming out of his shell. The adrenaline of the night might have shocked him back to life."

"Maybe." We walked across the road and began the ascent to the headland. "I'm just so glad that Wayne is paying for his crimes. I know he had a traumatic childhood, but people like that can't be allowed to roam free."

"I agree. And thanks to your gift, he won't." Riley held both bunches of flowers in one hand and draped his other arm around my shoulders.

"It was a team effort," I said.

"So, had any…visions, lately?" Riley inquired. "I mean, you don't have to tell me or anything, but I'm curious and fascinated. And if you ever want to tell me stuff, I'm here."

I smiled. "Nothing much, nothing major anyway."

"So you can't tell me what questions are going to be on my exam papers?"

"Ha, nice try. Even if I did find out, I wouldn't tell you." I elbowed him in the ribs.

"What about lottery numbers? Super Bowl winner? C'mon, show me some love!" He laughed.

"I'll show you some love." I stopped walking and grasped his chin with my free hand, pulling him in for a smooch.

"Eight," he said.

"Ooh, I'm getting there." I giggled.

A cool breeze followed us as we strolled up the hill. "I wish you didn't have to work tomorrow," I whined.

"I know."

"It sucks."

"Yeah. I can't wait till I can get out in the big wide world and start a career." His arm slipped down my back, and his hand slipped into mine so naturally and effortlessly like our bodies were having their own conversation without realizing it.

"What do you want to do? Lemme guess, something with sports?"

"Maybe. Depends on what I can do that can also earn me some money."

"School gym teacher?"

"Forget that. I don't want to spend even more years in a

school. Maybe I could start out as a personal trainer and go from there."

"You'd be great. And who knows, you might end up being one of the trainers on *The Biggest Loser* and become famous."

He laughed a deep throaty laugh that made me want to pull him close and nestle into his side in front of a magnificent sunset. God, what was getting into me? Getting all schmaltzy!

"I don't know if I want to be famous. But *you*, if people knew what you could do—"

"Don't even go there. Revealing my secret to one person is enough for now, thank you very much."

"Don't worry, my lips are sealed." His thumb and forefinger trailed across his lips.

"Actually, I wouldn't mind getting involved in something like sports psychology." I shrugged. "Could be interesting."

"Yes, you would be awesome at that!" Riley's voice oozed enthusiasm. "Hey, maybe we could join forces—Riley and Savannah, CEOs of Forever Fit, or something," he mused.

"Not a bad idea, actually," I replied. "But who knows what the future will hold?" Riley shot a glance at me and we burst out laughing.

We neared the cemetery and I looked across the row of headstones, which were silent, still, alone, except for one. Mr. Jenkins stood over a grave. He held a red rose in his hand and let it drop. Then his head turned in our direction. This time his gaze didn't freak me out, didn't make me think he was some weirdo. It only showed me how sad he was over his wife's death, and how lonely, how lost he was without her. His mouth turned up into a gentle smile, and his hand lifted and gave a single wave. We waved back, and I gave him a smile that said "Thank you," "I know how you feel," and "It'll be okay." Sometimes a smile could say more than words ever could. Like Mom's smile on stage when she finally got to perform again. They'd organized an encore performance of the play last weekend, three weeks after our traumatic experience, since it hadn't been able to conclude on the opening night. Her wide smile was relieved, proud, and powerful. It had showed me the sense of accomplishment she'd felt, and the empowering feeling that, although Wayne had scarred her heart, he hadn't scarred her soul. He hadn't stopped her from moving on and doing what she loved. He hadn't let his finale become hers.

"Here it is." Riley stopped in front of a double grave. My heart jolted a little upon seeing my name on the headstone. *Savannah*. Six months ago that could have been me. Someone could have been standing in front of *my* grave. But this was for Savannah Pearce. Mother, wife, daughter.

"Hey there, Mom." Riley knelt down and filled the flower grate with water from his bottle, and then arranged Gino's flowers into it.

Her name on the headstone seemed to sparkle, or was that the sun reflecting off it? It appeared brighter than the others. I couldn't see her spirit anywhere nearby, but I could feel her. I could sense that she was there, there for her son.

"I know flowers are a bit girly, Dad," Riley said, moving to the right. "But I have it on good authority, from a man that these would be perfect." He placed the flowers into the grate, his hand hesitating on their petals before he let go. Riley stood with his hand moving in an arc and his thumb pointing behind him. "Over and out."

My breath hitched in my throat at the memory of his

father's special sign, and I placed my arm around Riley's waist as we walked away, back to the pathway that followed the curve of the headland.

I stopped at the bench seat, the D.D. engraving still visible, and smiled. "Riley, meet Dad. Dad, meet Riley."

"It's an honor, Mr. Delcarta." Riley smiled back.

I untied the string from the bunch of gerberas, and as Riley held the posy close to the back of the bench, I threaded the string between the slats and tied the flowers to the seat. They might not last forever, but his memory would.

Our hands swung together as one as we walked the length of the pathway, curving around to where it started going downhill, when a strong urge to just stop took over, to take in the view and feel its peace. My eyes scanned the baby-blue horizon with its sparkling water and fluffy white clouds softening the sky. "It's so beautiful," I whispered.

"It is," said Riley, then he turned my body to face him. "And so are you."

"Aww, you're so cheesy." I smiled.

"But you love it, don't you?" he teased.

"Yeah, I love it."

Riley brushed a wisp of hair off my forehead. "And I love *you*." He wasn't teasing or joking this time; his eyes didn't blink, he didn't grin. He simply looked at me in a way that made me feel adored, accepted, cherished, loved.

A different kind of bubbly sensation rose within me. Not like the one I'd get before a vision, but something new. It told me that I also felt the words Riley had said. I knew I was young and had my whole life ahead of me, but I'd been through a lot in my short life and knew what was real and what wasn't. This was real. This was…

"I love you too." The words left my lips before I'd had the chance to process my feelings. Before I'd had a chance to protest or rationalize or dispute. Good thing too, because I didn't want to protest them. I wanted to surrender, succumb, and embrace them. Life was for living and every moment counted.

Gentle as the ocean breeze, Riley's lips swept across mine in a rhythmic caress that ebbed and flowed and cleansed and nourished. His hands combed through my hair, lifting and tousling, every nerve in my body tingling from his touch. One moment in time, one lifetime in the mind. I'd never forget this. Or him. No matter how life turned out down the track.

When he slowly pulled back, his warmth lingered on my lips like he'd never left. I looked up into his deep, dark eyes. "Now that, my dear, was a perfect ten."

• • •

We arrived at the entrance to Roach Place, and Riley plucked his phone from his pocket. "Just remembered something, hang on." He tapped at the screen then held the phone by his side. "Well, what a day, huh?"

"Yeah. It's been good."

He eyed his phone and shifted on the spot.

"So, I guess we should, get back home?" I gestured toward the small cul-de-sac.

"Um, yeah." He looked distant and made no effort to move.

My brow furrowed. Why was he acting strange? Was it the declaration of love? Was he regretting sharing his true feelings?

His phone beeped and his fast reflexes lifted the phone up instantly. He smiled. "Well, what are we waiting for?" He grabbed my hand and we turned into our street.

We stopped in the middle of the road between our two houses. "Hey, does your mom happen to have any of that delicious homemade lemonade at the moment?" Riley asked.

"Hoping to score some, eh?" I teased. "I told you, she makes it every Saturday morning; so unless my sisters have downed the lot, you should be in luck. Wanna come in for a bit?"

"I thought you'd never ask." He smiled and we walked up the porch steps.

I pushed open the door and walked in, wondering why everything was so dark. All the drapes were closed and the lights were off, but...hang on, what was all that stuff on the coffee table?

"Surprise!" Voices shouted and people sprung up from behind the couch, and I jumped backward. Riley grasped me by the shoulders from behind.

"Surprise, Savvy," he said.

My heart raced for a moment, and then a huge grin stretched across my face. "Oh my God, what is this? A party?"

Talia switched on the lights and a mirror ball lamp sparkled in the corner of the room, balloons bobbed around, and fairy lights and streamers arched across the roof and dazzled under the mantle of the fireplace-bookcase. My gaze glanced above the bookcase and landed on a hand-painted sign:

Happy Sweet Sixteenth and a Half, Savannah!

My heart swelled with joy. "This is all…for me?"

Mom came up and hugged me. "You never got to have a birthday party. And when you got out of the hospital, we were so intent on keeping you relaxed and calm we didn't even think, but now…well, I know it's not at the exact sixteen and a half mark, but close enough. You deserve to celebrate this milestone in your life, sweetheart."

"But Serena and Sasha, it was their birthday too."

"We had ours while you were living it up in the hospital, Sav," said Sasha. "So it wasn't much of a celebration with you in there, but at least we were awake."

"Yeah," Serena agreed. "This one's for you, sis."

I turned to Riley. "You knew about this?"

He nodded with a smug look of satisfaction.

"That's why you checked your phone, to see if they were ready for me!" I whacked him on the arm. "You guys got me good. I had no idea." I shook my head and smiled.

Serena started up some cruisy music, and Tamara pointed to the food displayed on the coffee table. "Well, dig in everyone."

There was a huge bowl of—I'm guessing—salt and vinegar chips, my favorite, a punch bowl with—without a doubt—Mom's homemade lemonade, and enough chocolate to feed a small country. Well, maybe a state. Okay, at least everyone in this room. There was also a pile of presents on the couch, and my hands itched to open them. Talk about spoiled. They'd set a high standard, raised the bar, and would have to go one up on this every year from now on. Nah, kidding.

I was about to dig in but stopped. "Hang on guys, there's one thing missing."

"Oh, what?" Talia said.

"I'm not exactly dressed for the occasion." I gestured to my damp, sporty getup and sand-filled trainers. "Give me a few minutes to get into something more…" I was about to say comfortable when I changed my mind. "Fun! Won't be long."

I scooted off to my bedroom and opened the closet I shared with my sisters, most of it taken up by Sasha's various ensembles. I opted for black leggings and a fashionably oversized off-the-shoulder purple top; it was the color of the irises that adorned the property overlooking the harbor. I hung long silvery glass beads around my neck and hooked on my onyx earrings. Though, something told me I wouldn't need protection from negative energies tonight. But hey, they matched my black leggings. I ruffled my tangled mess of hair and ran a comb through it, parted it on the side, swept a dark section across my forehead in a curve, and then fixed it with a spritz of Sasha's hair spray. I stole a raspberry lip gloss from her cosmetic bag and swiped it across my lips then pressed them together and apart with a pop.

Now for some shoes…or should I just go barefoot? I eyed my small collection and a giggle surfaced in my belly. I knew *exactly* what to wear. I slid my feet into the warm, soft, fluffy Cheshire cat slippers and appraised the result in the mirror. So it was a bit silly, but who cares? Riley had already seen me wear them, and we were just at home. He'd have to accept me for who I was—a competitive, psychic, teenage, aneurysm survivor with crazy slippers. *Take it or leave it, Volleyball Guy.* I chuckled to myself.

"What's taking you so long, Savvy?" Sasha called out from the living room. "Have you turned into *me* or something?" She laughed. "Hurry up. You don't want to keep your darling boyfriend waiting."

I laughed too. *Darling* boyfriend. That word, it sounded so…old. Reserved for married couples. Like Mom and Dad. The memory of that night reared its ugly head, and I recalled how I'd been about to open Dad's letter to Mom that I'd found in the shoebox. *My darling Rose.*

I stepped out of my room and glanced toward Mom's bedroom across the hall. One little lift of the finger to break that seal and I'd know what it contained. It might even give me a clue about his disappearance. My breath quickened with the anticipation, the desire to find out what lay inside those paper walls. My foot hesitated as it went to step closer to Mom's room, and then I turned my gaze toward the laughter and chatter in the living room.

It wasn't the right time.

I had to leave the past buried for now. Someday I'd find out what was in that envelope, but not today. Today wasn't about the past or the future; it was about the present. Oh, and also the presents on the couch waiting for me to tear them open. You couldn't blame a girl for being just a little greedy, right?

I walked slowly to the living room, savoring the moment. Mom handed out lemonade, Sasha danced and twirled, Tamara gobbled chips, Serena took photos, and Riley, well, he was arm-wrestling Talia on the coffee table.

My sixteenth birthday party…just how I'd imagined it, only six months later than planned. And I wouldn't be drooling over hot guys in movies that night, uh-uh. No need when the real life version was right there in my living room. I smiled, happiness warming me from the inside. This picture in front of me, this reality, it was the best sight I'd seen all year. And there was only one word for it: sweet.

I'D LIKE TO THANK my family and friends for supporting and encouraging my writing career, especially Mum and Dad, and my son and fellow writer, Jayden—I look forward to reading your acknowledgements one day!

Huge thanks to my agent, Joelle Delbourgo, for your expert advice and experience, and for believing in my writing. I'm grateful to be working with you.

And extra huge thanks to Mary Cummings and Diversion Books for saying "yes" to The Delta Girls and helping me to bring the series to life. I'm glad to be working with you and everyone at Diversion—including my editor Randall Klein, Sarah and Eliza in production, and Brielle and Hannah in marketing.

To those who encouraged my idea for The Delta Girls from the start, especially Alli Sinclair and Fiona Yuile who critiqued the full manuscript of *Sight* so I could make it better, and Serena Sandrin-Tatti who helped me edit the opening chapters—thanks! I'd also like to thank fellow writers Alli Sinclair (again) and Diane Curran for your friendship and our fun online chats when we should be writing, and the many writers I've come to know as friends who inspire me and are there for advice and feedback when needed.

And a special thank you to Cassie, James, and Tristan at Coffee Guru Kiama for serving me delicious hot chocolate and food while I write, and often letting me stay late so I can finish 'one more page'!

And lastly, thanks to you, the reader, for choosing this book.

CPSIA information can be obtained at www.ICGtesting.com
Printed in the USA
BVOW08s1400060316

439271BV00004B/124/P